Journey
to the
Motherland

LARRY UKALI JOHNSON-REDD

The Reading Glass
BOOKS

The Reading Glass Books
(888) 420-3050
www.readingglassbooks.com
fulfillment@readingglassbooks.com

ACKNOWLEDGMENTS

I would like to thank my late wife who spent many hours typing the first manuscript of this book. I would also like to thank all of the good Nigerians who made me feel welcome during my tours of service as a government lecturer in Benin City.

Many thanks also, to my In-laws who took care of me when I caught malaria.

I would like to dedicate this book to my late wife, my family especially my mother and to all Black people in the U.S.A.; in fact, all African people on earth. I would like to dedicate this book to my 3 brothers who taught me so much about computers while we developed this edition. I would like to dedicate this book to my sister and her Nigerian husband, Harrison and Ann Oyedele. I would also like to dedicate this book to my other 2 sisters Sharon and her husband James Brown and Sandra and her daughter Nakita.

I would like to dedicate this book to a victim of police brutality, the late Larry D. Lumpkin and two late brothers I grew up with namely Brother Hakika and Brother Ayantuga Olade these brothers died in Nigeria in the early 1980's, I sat with them in 1979 while visiting the USA and we discussed Nigeria at length that afternoon. Finally I would like to dedicate this book to all of my ancestors on all sides of our family. I would also like to dedicate this book to all of my uncles, aunts and cousins in North Little Rock Arkansas and the Bay Area. I grew up with Ayan and Hakika in San Francisco's Lakeview area. I also want to dedicate this book to all my people all over the world.

This book is also dedicated to my namesakes, my father who raised me from as long as I can remember, the late Mr. Henry Redd Sr. and my father who made me and whom I got to know very well, the late Mr. Elijah Johnson as well as my grandmothers and grandfathers. Lastly I would dedicate this book to Yvette.

In 2017 I also want to extend my dedication to all students I have taught or administered while I was a school administrator or teacher. I also extend this dedication of this book to my family, extended family, cousins and friends and Katrina.

PREFACE

The turbulent days of Black Civil Rights struggle witnessed in America in the early sixties, may have come and gone. The Black Nationalist movements of the Organization of Afro American Unity (OAAU), led by Malcolm X, of blessed memory, may have become a thing of the past. But the conditions against which the various struggles were waged have not completely disappeared.

That factor has given rise to the emergence of some smaller groups, as well as solo efforts like that of The Black Expatriate. But wait a minute, what is a black expatriate? Expatriates are most certainly known to be whites; at least in the African context. * Never mind that Nigerians have been known to become expatriates up in Northern Nigeria because only whites are known to be qualified for whatever position they occupy.

Next, you hear that The Black Expatriate is a book. What kind of book can it be and what would it be talking about? Before you know it, you are talking to a Fulani-looking six-footer of a man. He introduces himself, but quickly insists that you call him Ukali. You don't understand. Is he thinking that Ukali is easier for you to pronounce or what? "No," he says. He adds that his name is a name of someone his grandparents worked for as slaves. For example, every black who worked on Smith's plantation became known as Smith.

*An Expatriate is a person who resides and works in a foreign country.

"The Black Expatriate...," I started wanting to slip in a question, but Ukali would not let me. He cut in: "1 have been in Nigeria now for two years, and the experiences I have had, have been very challenging. It is definitely unique in many ways and I felt that these were the kind of experiences that could lead to a positive black story."

He adds that he has therefore written The Black Expatriate to try to correct the many, many wrong impressions whites have created in the minds of Afro- Americans about Africa and Africans.

Ukali feels that there should be more communication between all the Black peoples of the world. ',It is in this direction that I have attempted to tell the story of a Black American's experiences in Africa," he says.

(Excerpt from "Meet The Black Expatriate", Spear Magazine, December 1979, written by Ide Eguabor.)

TABLE OF CONTENTS

FEELING GOOD IN AFRICA

Family we are forever
We survive any weather
In our people's land
Home of the Black Man
My friend Pat Finn
Bought the drink
I am free
I can think
I'm feeling good in Africa
So good in Africa
In Black Africa
My people's Africa
Where sisters do what is good
And brothers carve from black wood
Here we are in Africa
Black People's Africa
Where a Black Government
Is the master of development
Many she-goats and rams
And afternoon traffic jams
Don't ask for me
In ole Frisco
If you're cool
You will know
I'm feeling good in Africa
So good in Africa
In Black Africa
My people's Africa

CHAPTER 1

Feeling Good in Africa

We arrived at the Immigration Office early that morning. I turned into the narrow driveway and parked in the parking lot at the rear of the building. We climbed the stairs up to the office, and introduced ourselves to the officer who was seated at the far side of the office. After viewing my passport, the officer said that I did not have a valid visa. He explained further that I was supposed to report my presence in the country and obtain an alien registration card. He also said that my visa had expired.

I told the brother, who was in his early thirties, that I had neglected to read that portion of my passport. He asked, "Why are you reporting now, two years after your arrival in the country, instead of within 21 days of your arrival? It is stated right here in your passport." I explained to him that I had had a hard time adjusting to the country initially. That was part of it. The other part was that I felt like I was at home all the time and so I did not think of myself as being an alien. He looked me dead in the eye and wondered if I was sincere in what I was saying. My wife interjected that I would need the re-entry permit and a resident visa so that we could proceed on vacation. The man focused his attention in her direction and asked: "When do you plan to leave?" She gave a date and the mood of the man changed as the frown disappeared from his face and he expressed his desire to cooperate.

I had tuned out of the conversation, looking around at the ceiling fan that was at work My eyes covered every inch of the walls. I heard the word 'cooperate' and rejoined the conversation. He gave us instructions and said that if we meet them 'in time', everything would be all right. He warned us on the seriousness of the situation and then smiled.

We began doing all we could to meet the conditions. The first task involved obtaining an alien registration card. The registration card took three days to obtain, however, in the process; we met a nice brother who helped us to solve another outstanding problem. Once we had received the alien registration card, I obtained the necessary form letter from my job that would be needed along with the other things that the officer in the Immigration Office wanted.

Once we had met all the necessary conditions, we drove down Sapele Road to the Immigration Office. We met the officer and gave him our papers. He examined the papers, making sure that everything was complete. He then asked, "When do you people want to go?" We told him our departure date and he asked us to come back the following day.

It was now time to face the red tape that was to be faced at the Education Board and the Bank. It turned out to be as frustrating as I thought it would be. We finished all of our business Thursday afternoon, just in time to make final preparations for a Friday morning departure from Benin City.

We worked hard at packing throughout the night and early that morning and arrived at the airport at 9:20, which were just a few minutes before the flight was closed. Although we were told that we were late, the jet did not arrive from Lagos for some hours to come. The time passed by quickly as we filled ourselves with Shish Kebab "Congo meat" and Star Beer. At about 1:30 p.m. that afternoon, we found ourselves rushing to the tarmac to meet a Lagos bound jet.

As the jet began to move, I captured one last glance at Benin City and I thought about all Benin City meant to me.

The jet pointed its nose to the sky and began its ascent. I looked at the jet, a 737 that was packed with black-faced travelers. The flight was quick and uneventful, as we were already alighting from the jet within thirty minutes from takeoff from Benin City.

Lagos was its old self. There was evidence of rain and a small drizzle sprinkled on the passengers who were running for the lounge and the baggage-claim area.

We made our way to the baggage-claim area and of course, we were pounced upon by the taxi drivers who were ready for a new passenger. I had gone through the routine many times before, and after a short wait, the workers in the baggage-claim area brought the first load of baggage. We received all of our baggage, which we put on a cart, and proceeded to the exit door. When we got to the exit door, one well-dressed young man whispered that his taxi was a 504 Peugeot with a cassette, and therefore he would offer us a comfortable ride. I had not decided which taxi I wanted to take, but I decided to follow the underdog.

The driver of the car we rode in was not the same guy who hustled us in the baggage-claim area of the airport. The guy who hustled us was an agent of the driver. He looked so dignified in his traditional outfit, I thought he was 'cool'. The car we drove away in turned out to be a Volkswagen Gala, a private car, as, many car owners use their Private cars as taxis in Lagos.

The jet pointed its nose to the sky and began its ascent. I looked at the jet, a 737 that was packed with black-faced travelers. The flight was quick and uneventful, as we were already Alighting from the jet within thirty minutes from takeoff from Benin City.

This Volkswagen Igala was barely moving, with the engine virtually straining itself, and jumping from first gear to second gear. The clouds began to recede and the sun began to shed light on Ikeja, a city located north-Capital. Lagos. Ikeja is where the west of airports are located west of the Capital, Lagos. Ikeja is where my wife's cousin and her handsome husband live. They are our favorite people in Lagos. Update: the Federal Capital has been moved to Abuja in the center of the country.

Although we arrived unannounced, we met the traditional African hospitality. The taxi-driver and his conductor put up a fuss about the fare, but we knew they were happy with what we had given them. They left when they realized that our hosts were old-timers in Lagos, therefore, they could not cheat us.

We met our hosts enjoying a mid-afternoon lunch, and I remembered that it is impolite to refuse food offered. So we joined them after a bottle of Guilder Beer. My favorite soup; egwusi was being served with eba. A basin of water was brought to the table; we washed our hands and enjoyed the meal the African way.

I felt so good after the food and beer that I felt sleep creeping upon me. My hosts noticed that I was sleepy and prepared their guestroom, so that I could take a nap. The time passed by quickly, and before long, I scrambled to my feet. I realized that I had worked too hard, the night before, with sleep escaping my gasp. I washed up after my nap and sat down in the beautifully furnished living room, and watched television. Richard was there, and in no time our conversation moved from the program on the television to the upcoming elections. Theresa emerged from the kitchen with rice and stew, saying, "Come and eat because travelers should eat well." The food we had eaten earlier was not fully digested; however, I felt that we should go ahead and eat the piping-hot food that smelled so good.

We all sat down at the table to eat the good food that Africa's land and my in- laws' efforts had produced. After the meal, we moved back to the living room where the evening news was already showing on television. The clock was moving steadily and before long, it was time to start going to the airport.

This time however, we would not be going to the small Domestic Airport, but to the newly commissioned Muratala Muhammad International Airport. Night was upon Ikeja, and by it being a Saturday, I knew many people would be prancing and dancing to the black beat of Reggae, Afro-Beat, Soul and Juju Music. We drove past the Domestic Airport; the little used old International Airport, towards the new Muratala Muhammed International Airport, in my in-laws' comfortable car. We finally spotted the road that would lead up to the new airport. The new airport was lit up like the brightest lights on Broadway. It was a massive chunk of western Technology resting on African land. One glance let me know that it was second to none anywhere in the world. It was beautiful. We drove up the departure ramp and unloaded our luggage, entered the airport only to be impressed with the cleanliness and newness of the ticket counters. The shining steel beams and glass that covered the front of the airport, held our attention until we realized that the time to board was near.

Our luggage was loaded on to the scales at the Nigerian Airways ticket counter. The weight of our luggage was within the limits, so we brought our remaining carry-on luggage to the Customs counter for checking and we were cleared. In no time, with the Customs Officers' working quickly, we finished with our paperwork in no time, and finally made it up to the gate from which we would board. All of the passengers lined up so that boarding passes could be collected.

There was a short delay, however, which afforded me the opportunity to speak to a gentleman who was also bound for New York. He was a Nigerian, however, I did not discuss business with him. The line was formed again and this time, I opened my eyes and noticed that all of the passengers were black.

As our boarding passes were being collected, I took my last look at the shining steel beams and the newness of the airport, before handing in my boarding pass to the beautiful stewardess. I was impressed by the fact that Black people could run the airport so smoothly. As we started walking towards the jet, we were surprised by a group of airport guards, who made a quick search of our person. As a young airport guard padded me down, I noticed that a gentleman, smartly dressed in a national dress, was in a small cubical trying to explain something to the two guards who stood on both sides of him.

There was no rush and we took our seats in the economy section. The passengers were all seated and after a short delay, some more crew members entered the jet and the doors to the big jet were closed. We taxied to the runway and made a smooth take-off.

I looked out the window, taking my final glances at Nigeria. I could see the bush, the trees, some swamps, the countryside, and the Atlantic Ocean, as the jet carried us beyond Ikeja. As the journey began, I wondered if my people, - the Afroans* had liberated themselves. I thought about how my peoples' dreams for freedom had been shattered by the disrespect of our dignity. My wife and I talked for a while. It was now 11:00 p.m. by Nigerian time and my wife felt sleepy. In no time, she was asleep. My thoughts went back to the Afroans; the Africans born in America. I wondered if Jim Crow would ever let go I wondered whether my people continued to suffer racial discrimination in housing, employment, and all of the other areas. I wondered if the young brothers were still unemployed. I remembered how young Afroans who were at the bottom of society were still referred to as unemployable. My thoughts were interrupted by the announcement by the pilot that we would be landing In Monrovia, Liberia, shortly.

*Afroan is author's nomenclature for Afro-American.

The jet began its descent and skypower gave us a nice smooth landing. Our jet was among only a few jets in our view. As the jet lay waiting for the Liberian passengers to board, I thought about the recent rice riots in Liberia. I thought that I could tell the 'Congo' people or Amerce-Liberians apart from the 'Country' people when they boarded the jet.

We were on the ground for about 45 minutes before the new passengers began to board. Some were dressed in the traditional African attire, while others boarded in suits and ties. As I looked at their faces, I found out that it was impossible to distinguish between whom was who. I could not be sure that the brother or sister who wore a Dashiki or a Wrapper was not a Congo or Americo Liberian. I could not be sure if those wearing suits and dresses were not Country Liberians. I wondered why it is that the useless distinction existed at all.

Most of the Liberians were speaking African languages and they seemed to be traveling as a group or a tour. The sound of voices coming from all corners of the jet must have comprised the major languages of Nigeria and Liberia.

The jet, full of black faces, was finally ready to take off. Skypower took to the air, ready for a Trans-Atlantic flight. Once the cabin leveled out, the stewardesses and flight attendants went through their well rehearsed safety speech.

It was 12:00 a.m. by my watch, which had been set on Nigerian time. I could look below in the black of night at what I knew was the Atlantic Ocean. I thought how rough this same Trans-Atlantic trip must have been for my ancestors, many whose bones lay at the bottom of the Atlantic.

I thought of many things without coming to any conclusions. I began to feel sleepy. Whatever the time was, I knew I wanted to sleep. My woman was already asleep. Suddenly, my mind flashed back to the earliest days of my life. My mind journeyed through time until I started thinking about what happened after my junior high school graduation. I felt sleep creeping upon me. My dream for the night was set.

CHAPTER 2

After Graduation

Many new realities revealed themselves to me after the graduation exercise. Many of my friends did not graduate on that day and many more would go to Lowell High School and Lincoln High School. The schools in The City (San Francisco), are built in the various neighborhoods, the district one lives in determines which school one attends.

My friends who were accepted into Lowell like all of Lowell's students, had to have a special recommendation from the Principal of the previous school, as well as a very high academic record. To tell the truth, few Afroans were accepted into Lowell. It was initially the last white city high school; however, San Francisco's Asian Community changed the character of Lowell High School.

My friends who lived in the district for Lincoln High School, felt that they were the people most likely to have a good time in high school. I lived in the district for Balboa High School. Balboa had a large Afroan student population and a tough reputation. Aptos Junior High School, the school I was graduating from, was a predominantly white school. Ninety percent of the students were white, ninety five percent of the teaching staff was white, while all the administrators were all white. The only black staff were the Janitors and the kitchen employees.

As I was standing on the stage ready to accept my Junior High School diploma, I wondered if I had made the right choice to cut my hair. You see, I had grown an Afro, but the Afro cut had not really become popular by the time I had cut my hair for that graduation. However, I promised myself that I would let it grow back during the summer.

I was very happy when the ceremony was over. I did not like my junior high school, nor the Boys' Dean, the Principal, etc.

I looked forward to attending a school where there would be more black students. I was not scared by the rumors that were floating around, about how bad Balboa High School would be. In Aptos Junior High School, the number of black students was small, and so was the choice of girls. I looked forward to attending a high school that would be full of fine sisters. Many of the other brothers at Aptos developed a complex and felt they could only chase white girls. That was not my 'bag'.

Aptos Junior High School was an old school in a white neighborhood of San Francisco. It was no surprise that the student population of the school was predominantly white. In the mornings, we reported to our Home Room, roll would be taken, and school announcements were made and discussed. Black students were limited to five or so per classroom and there were special classes for the blacks who were yet to master English. Many of my friends were in those classes and the fact that they were branded 'slow learners' meant nothing without realizing that after 400 years, American English is not the first language of the Afroans. Afroan English is understood by all Afroans, even the ones who have learned to say: "1 like my meat rare." My parents had one habit of forcing all of us to watch the news every night. They tried to see to it that we were educated. As children, we only wanted to look at movies or cartoons. Oftentimes, children blank out their minds to anything they do not want to watch. This summer was no exception at its onset. It was 1967, and this was the fourth long, hot summer in a row. The first one began in 1964; the second long, hot summer began in 1965 in Watts, Los Angeles, California. By 1966, the long, hot summers had become an institution.

The long, hot summers were uprisings by Afroans, fed up with suffering the effects of Jim Crowism. In previous summers, I would always be on the baseball field, when the news was on. That time, my hope in life was to be a professional baseball player. During my three years of junior high school, I was not selected for the school team. It did not alter my confidence in my ability to play, however, I did not realize that if you are a brother, you have to be a super star to make the teams; whereas if one is a white boy, one can make the team even if he is less than average.

The summer of 1967, was no different from the previous long hot summers. Everyday, the news was full of stories of the Black uprisings. I began to follow the events on the TV, and suddenly, San Francisco began to experience uprisings.

The Afroan rebellion sprang up in city after city. The high schools, colleges and university campuses, became battle grounds. Most of the rebellions began as a spontaneous reaction to racist police brutality. I say racist because ninety percent of the police are white and the victims are Afroans.

The television captured the viciousness of the situation, and from that point on, my sympathies for my people began to grow. Racial tensions began to grow.

The sight of brothers and sisters being battered with 'Nigger knockers', opened my eyes. 'Nigger knockers' as they called them, were long hardwood sticks that the police used as batons. Unlike the smaller batons, these 'nigger knockers' were up to three feet long.

As the long, hot summer of 1967, drew to an end, my thoughts were focused on the first day of high school at Balboa High. Balboa had a reputation of being lone of the roughest high schools in The City.

I reflected on how my elementary school classroom which, at one point, had only five blacks and by the time I was about to graduate, that same classroom had only five whites. Junior high school was also a white trip full of peril; after all, they were ninety percent of the school population. My thoughts then returned to reality. Reality was that Balboa High School would not be all black, however, Balboa appeared to be a black-majority school. If one was to look at the year book, this fact would be doubted, however, many brothers and sisters were not around by the end of the school year.

After graduation, many events transpired without making an impact. Malcolm X was assassinated in February 21, 1965. The Harlem uprising and many other events took place, however, it was the long, hot summer of 1967, that caused the beginning of my awakening.

CHAPTER 3
The First Day and the Movement

September, 1967

My first day at Balboa High School started off smoothly. I attended my classes, happy to see so many Afroans ; some of my classes were majority black, however, many were not. I was enchanted to see so many beautiful well-dressed sisters. I found my way around to all of my classes, asking the various sisters for directions. My older brother was already in the school, but I felt I did not need to be led around by the nose. The fact that he was a senior and a participant in school activities kept him very busy.

The whites in Balboa were different from the ones at my junior high school, as they were children of working class or lower whites. However, at Aptos, the whites were elites or children of white socialites. The Afroans at Balboa were descendants of the 'Field Niggers', whereas, at Aptos, Afroans tried to fit into the 'House Nigger' mold.

I took the bus from our house located on the Mount Davidson side of Lakeview district. The school day had passed without an incident. I met many of my elementary school mates and some friends who had always attended schools, other than the one I had attended. I decided to walk home on the first day. I did not know the quickest or shortest way to go, however, most of the Afroars lived in Lakeview. I decided to follow the path that many were taking around the front of the school, then down to San Jose Street, San Jose Street to Mount Vernon Street, which led me home.

I could smell racial tension in the air at the school. I walked to the front of the school as classes were over. I had survived my first day. All of a sudden, I noticed that on the side of the street where the school was located, there stood about fifty brothers, who all had pocket knives.

I noticed that on the other side of the street, there stood about fifty or so white boys all heavily armed with lead pipes, long sticks, broken bottles, and knives. The whites who lived in the surrounding neighborhood took advantage of the fact that the school was located in the middle of a white community, by collecting heavier weapons than the black students. As I scanned the brothers, the stern look on their faces let me know that they did not want a first-day student in their way. I moved away from this hot spot I had stumbled into. Once I was away from the campus, some of my friends informed me about what had taken place in school, that had caused the trouble. Some whites had been in a fight with some brothers and each group had called friends for help. That stand-off ended without trouble.

I spent the next few weeks making adjustments to my new situation. I had to learn my way around the big school. All students were assigned lockers for their books and other school materials. The locks were combination locks, so I had to memorize my locker combination. The racial tension that was at a high pitch the first day, had died down, but it did not fade away.

Some of the Afroan juniors and seniors wanted to form a club. It was going to be called the Afro-American Club. It was open for membership to the school, however, unofficially, it was open to black students only, In order to have a club in that school, the students had to have a faculty member as sponsor, The Afro-American Club convinced one black Biology teacher (the only black man on the teaching staff) to sponsor the club. I decided to go to one of their meetings to see what was happening.

The Afro-American Club was made up of seniors and juniors mainly, and their interest primarily, focused on identifying with the emerging black culture. I felt good to participate in the meeting, although I felt that the club lacked dynamism.

This was not the situation at the San Francisco State University. A Black Student Union was formed there and those brothers and sisters were together. The B.S.U. at State had identified itself with the rebellion and the movement in the Black Community. Some of the top members were identified with the Black Panther Party.

The school year at Balboa was coming to an end. The members of the Afro- American Club wanted to change the name to the Black Student Union like the brothers and sisters at San Francisco State University, who established the first B.S.U. in the San Francisco area.

This was seen as a bold move by the school authorities. They feared that society's trouble would find its way into the classrooms. In fact, the Black Power Movement had entered the classroom with the Afros (Naturals) that sat like a mountain of pride on top of our heads.

Black Power had become a part of those Afroans who were willing to make waves, rebel, and fight for freedom of the Black race. Black Power caused young Afroans to ask their white history teachers to teach the truth about Africans, and to add relevant African History books to the school library.

Balboa was the first high school to establish a Black Student Union among San Francisco high schools. The members of the Afro-American Club had become members of the Black Student Union. The sponsor remained the same the lone black biology teacher. My participation in the new Black Student Union finally put me in trouble.

The Black Student Union wanted to put up a school announcement. It read: "Brothers and Sisters, you are all invited to a B.S.U. meeting this Thursday." I was among those that put up the first announcement. It caused quite a stir. The student government did not approve of the announcement before it was put up and before the student government could make a decision, the Principal pulled down the announcement.

The moderate B.S.U. leadership was at an impasse. The members who were young, wanted to make a case about the announcement being removed, while other social clubs had their announcements all over the school. At Thursday's meeting, the brothers and sisters were angry and confronted our sponsor. He explained what the Principal had told him. The Principal said that the B.S.U. could not be an all-Black organization, that it must be open to all students.

The Principal also said that since the poster read: 'Brothers and Sisters...' that it meant only Blacks were invited, however, the sponsor countered the Principal's argument by telling us that all unions refer to their members as brothers and sisters. The B.S.U. decided to use this argument. The general feeling of the B.S.U. was that it should remain an all-Black organization. The confrontation over the announcement made the B.S.U. popular among Black Students.

I took time on a Saturday to go and listen to a speech by a revolutionary brother. I accompanied my friend to the meeting. When we arrived, I knew I was not in a strange place. I saw many of my classmates from Aptos Junior High School and many from Balboa. I was spellbound for three hours as the brother spoke on all aspects of the Black Liberation Struggle. I returned to that same place many times after that for numerous meetings. At the meetings I met many beautiful revolutionary Afroans.

After some time, the meetings were no longer held in Lakeview, but switched to the Fillmore. Fillmore district was a part of San Francisco that I did not know well, so I had reservations about going there. Everyone in San Francisco remembered how Lakeview, Fillmore and Hunters' Point used to be before the Black Power Movement. Lakeview boys dared not enter any part of Fillmore or Hunters' Point. District gangs were formed and they attacked anyone they found in their area from another district.

I found myself happy to go to the Fillmore with some of the brothers in the organization. There was no problem. We traveled down Fillmore from Church Street down to Geary Street. On the way, we stopped at Lenard's Barbeque Pit to eat. The barbeque was very good. After touring the Fillmore I had no fear of entering the Fillmore anymore. I joined the movement in the Fillmore.

The movement for African-American liberation was happening in the sixties (1960's). African-Americans were marching, protesting, agitating and pushing for our rights. The sixties was like the Black Renaissance of the 1920's led by Marcus Garvey and many others.

Many brothers and sisters wore Afros or naturals, dyshikies, black leather coats along with combat boots and Black Power Salutes replaced the gang war attitudes prevalent even in the early 1960's.

Many brothers were throwing down their lives and dieing in Vietnam in a "White Man's War and returning with ak47 assault rifles to face racial discrimination and police brutality. The struggle for our liberation began 400 years ago. In the sixties there were many instances of police brutality such as the murder of Mathew Johnson which began the riots and rebellion in the San Francisco Hunters Point African-American community. This rebellion ended when the police withdrew and the National Guard were deployed.

CHAPTER 4
The Takeover

One day, while riding to Fillmore for a meeting, we discussed the idea of taking over the B.S.U.; after all, the seniors were more interested in graduating off the stage. In fact, every time there was a confrontation, the school authorities only had to threaten graduating members who made up the B.S.U. leadership. I was a low junior then, and since all of my friends were also first and second year students, we hatched a plan to overthrow the leadership. To us, it was a matter of taking the leadership out of the hands of those who were only interested in graduating. Our group was Interested in fighting for Black Liberation.

The following Monday, we began informing our classmates of the need for dynamic leadership within the B.S.U. Our classmates accepted this analysis and plans were formulated for the takeover. The takeover was not a personal trip against any member of the present leadership. Somewhere friends we had known over the years. The takeover movement gained momentum and students began attacking the present leadership for their lack of dynamism.

The argument against the lack of dynamism turned into a campaign against the seniors. The juniors and Sophomores felt that the seniors who constituted the B.S.U. leadership were only interested in staying on sweet terms with the all-white school administration. the B.S.U. originated from a need for justice. It had to be dynamic and stand up to the school administrators, and tell them the feelings, grievances and needs of Afroan students.

A target date for removing the B.S.U. leadership was set. It would be at the Thursday meeting after school. As usual, the meeting would take place in our sponsor's science classroom, as all of the science classrooms were bigger than the regular classrooms. All of the militant Black students were anxiously waiting for the upcoming meeting. As the day grew closer, one could see that changing the B.S.U. leadership was the only available path. Many brothers and sisters from Lakeview, Hunters' Point, and Sunnydale, made promises to be there.

Thursday morning arrived and though the target date had arrived, the school authorities had not made any move to block our action. In fact, the B.S.U. leadership was so involved with senior class activities, that they did not even know what was happening. The leadership was not made up of Uncle Toms, but their status was what made them pliable. At that time, seniors never thought of doing anything that would prevent them from going to senior activities.

As the school day ended, I was among the first people to arrive at the science classroom. I had a big stake in the success of the takeover; I, as a low junior would be the new B.S.U. President! Many brothers and sisters began pouring into the room. The ones who would occupy other positions in the B.S.U. were already there and ready. Suddenly, I realized that the two top leaders, the President and the Vice President were not present. How could that be? This was an important meeting, and a regularly scheduled one.

My first thought was that they had been informed about what would take place at the meeting. Then, one brother informed me that there were senior activities going on that day in another school, and that our seniors were there. They did not notify anyone that they would be unable to show up for the B.S.U. meeting, even though they had conducted all of the meetings up until that day.

Suddenly, one brother said, "Now is the time." We sat in the front of the room and I opened the meeting by saying: "Our President is away. Since this is a meeting to remove him, he does not have to be present." Many people began to raise their hands to be allowed the chance to speak. Some made statements against the present leadership, while others said that it was time for a change.

Usually, B.S.U. meetings were attended regularly by twenty to twenty-five students. On this nice Thursday afternoon, seventy brothers and sisters squeezed into the room. They were mainly juniors and sophomores with a few militant seniors. More and more of the brothers and sisters were airing their views. There was general agreement on what had to be done.

I took a long, deep breath and said: "It is time for new elections." Many brothers and sisters said, "Right On" with very loud voices. I continued: "It is time for this B.S.U. to have dynamic revolutionary leadership." I asked, "If you feel like I do, let me know by saying 'Right On'." What followed was a thunderous 'Right On' by the brothers and sisters. I asked that I be made President. I announced the names of those who would constitute the new leadership. I asked the brothers and sisters to raise up their hands in the Black Power salute. It was a unanimous decision. I said, "Brothers and Sisters, the leadership will take over as of right now!" Many were showing their approval by shouting 'Right On' and 'Black Power'.

At this opportune moment, the former President and former Vice President of the B.S.U., entered the classroom. They were greeted by boos and jeers. Some people were calling them Toms. The President spoke first, saying that any elections held at that time were considered null and void. The Vice President concurred. I was put on the spot, as I had known the President for many years. He was making a last ditch effort to save a position he really did not want.

I kept quiet, in order to give the brothers and sisters a chance to do what they felt. Shouts from the audience were directed to the two seniors. By that time, the room had become highly tense. Many were saying, "Shut up! Where were you, when we needed you? There were more Screams "Sit down seniors; your days are over. The atmosphere in the room showed the two seniors that there was no hope and finally, they gave up and left in shame. After the speech, there were loud applause of 'Right On', ringing all over the room as the meeting was adjourned.

CHAPTER 5

The Day They Lied

The Black Students Union at Balboa High School began to grow after the takeover. All of the meetings were well attended. The brothers and sisters were happy to see that the B.S.U. was functioning so well. Many Afroan Students were being suspended and victimized, however, the power of our unity was so great, that the authorities began to take note. Occasionally, a crisis would erupt. Balboa was a racial powder keg that could blow up at any time.

One incident occurred after a rumor was spread that two white male students had attacked and injured a sister. It was lunchtime at Jacks, the restaurant opposite the main entrance and exit of the school which the Afroans used as a hangout. Afroans naturally group together and congregate at any cool location. Tension and fear entered Jacks with the story of the injured sister. I happened to be at Jacks because, I loved squeezing in and out of the little hot spot full of fine sisters. I had finished buying my lunch, while speaking with some of the sisters. The place was too crowded to eat, so, slowly, I made my way towards the door, touching all the black beauty I could.

Then, without a word of warning, I saw one sister pull a hand full of hair, and that person hit the ground. Jacks, all of a sudden became a racial powder keg, and sisters began grabbing and beating non-Afroans in the tightly packed hot spot.

I managed to get out of Jacks with my food. It was a conflict strickly between sisters and their racial counterparts, so I did not get Involved. Once outside, I started eating my lunch in a hurry. I could sense trouble. I wanted to go around the corner where many of the brothers usually sit, on the stairs of the houses of the people who lived adjacent to the school. What I met, once there, was a group of highly upset brothers. These brothers were from Sunnydale and Hunters' Point, although some were from Lakeview. I walked up and asked, "What is this?" The brothers replied: "It is time for a fist rally. Our sister has been beaten and the school authorities have not done anything about it."

Many of the brothers I saw that day were among those who put me in office. It was obvious that there would be no school that afternoon. Some of the brothers said that this should be a B.S.U. sponsored fist rally. I know that if there was B.S.U. backing, the rally would close down the school for sure. I did not want to play the last card at the first encounter with school authorities, so said, "This place is not our community, so if the trouble were to become intensified, we could be trapped."

The school authorities had notified the police that a riot was in progress, and the school was declared closed. The police advanced on the areas where brothers and sisters were and began chasing the Afroan students with their long sticks which they call 'nigger knockers'. Soon, we found ourselves on the run towards home.

School resumed one week later and tension had eased up No doubt, the trouble in the society- the riots, rebellions and rallies, had entered society's miniature form - the school. The term passed by quickly, as we tried hard to catch up with the schoolwork missed because of the unscheduled holidays. The B.S.U. meetings were well attended and since some of the:: heroes of past fighting were members in good standing,; the B.S.U. maintained a powerful image. A popular Black football player was elected Student Body President, however, he was not involved in the B.S.U. He had his image as Student Body President to maintain.

The first term ended and as we started the second semester we had a firm grip on the B.S.U.. It was February and the memorial date of the assassination of Malcolm X was coming close.

On the Thursday of the first week in the term, we had a B.S.U. meeting. At the meeting, it was suggested that we organize a memorial for our fallen leader. Most of us were too young to understand Malcolm X at the time of his assassination in 1965, however, Malcolm's uncompromising stand for the Black Peoples' of the world, earned our greatest respect.

The following week went by very quickly. We were busy with schoolwork, and busy planning our memorial. The B.S.U. wanted to have a guest speaker, who would speak on the life and philosophy of Malcolm X. It was not unusual for student organizations to sponsor rallies that were attended by the entire student body. Finally, we were ready to present our plan to the Principal of the school.

The Principal, a tricky, old man and veteran of World War II, was the fifth Principal during my first two years of high school. He was determined not to be driven away from the school by the outbreak of racial hostility. He asked us why we stuck to saluting each other with a clenched fist, and went on to say that a clenched fist represented Nazism. We informed him that Black Power had no connection with Nazism. We went on to inform the Principal that the memorial for Malcolm X would be conducted in an orderly manner. He would not agree to have a two-section memorial assembly, that would encompass the whole school. Instead, he agreed to open the auditorium at both lunch periods only, as a compromise. He said that our memorial assembly could take place at that time only, and that students who wished could attend.

Immediately after that, we began to plan the memorial. We contacted our main guest speaker, a renowned Black Power advocate, and other Community groups like R.A.P(Rally of African American Parents), a group of concerned Afroan parents, was also invited.

On Wednesday, the day before the rally, the Principal called the B.S.U. leadership for a meeting. At the Meeting, the principal said that the memorial assembly was going to be cancelled because he feared bringing people from our community into the school. We reminded the principal that many of the community people were parents of students in the school. This was to no avail. The principal maintained his position and told us he had to follow orders. To us this was a quick way to discredit the BSU to the Black students and to show that the school authorities had their hatred for Malcolm X and all that he represented. This was their position but our position was that Malcolm X was the most dynamic Afroan political scientist in our time.

That evening, there was a meeting of the Central Committee of the B.S.U. in a secret location. This bold act by the Principal of agreeing and then disagreeing about the memorial, had put the credibility of the B.S.U. on the line. Something had to be done to show the school authorities that we would not accept double standards. The Central Committee which was made up of many dynamic brothers and sisters, held a serious meeting as plans were hatched to hold the memorial, in spite of the fast talking Principal.

I could not wait for the next day to come, as I was determined to make a stand. I thought about the consequences, but I knew that I would be involved in some trouble, whatever the outcome. The die was cast.

Early the next day, all of the Central Committee members met at the agreed time. We split up into different columns. I accompanied two brothers to the cafeteria where late students were during the first period of school. When we started walking, I noticed more and more brothers and sisters joining the protest march. We were about twelve by then marching to battle. Suddenly, we came upon 'No Neck'. That was the name we had given to the Boys' Dean because his head sat squarely on his body.

'No Neck' looked at our delegation with scorn and hatred. He noticed that I, the B.S.U. President was at the head, leading the delegation. There was no destruction of property, only a test of will. 'No Neck' looked at me and said, "Come over here." I felt the blood rush through my body as I went up to him, however, the spirit of the delegation offered me inspiration. 'No Neck' said that I should come and talk with him privately, no doubt, he had a trick up his sleeve. I kept my distance from him, because I felt that the delegation and what it represented meant more to me than 'No Neck'. I positioned myself where 'No Neck' could hear me.

'No Neck' looked at me with a stern face and said, "Do you know what you are doing?" I said, "Yes. The B.S.U. is going to have the memorial for our hero, the late Malcolm X, one way or the other." 'No Neck' became furious for many reasons, and his face turned red. I could see hatred and scorn in his eyes. In a threatening voice, he said, "If you don't stop immediately with this nonsense, you will be suspended for disrupting school activities."

The threat had been taken seriously, as the voice of Malcolm X began to speak to me like a secret message. I must have been thinking about his records, Message to the Grassroots or Ballots or Bullets. When I thought about how much my people had lived under the threat of intimidation, this new intimidation had to be challenged! I looked at 'No Neck', whom we all felt was an oppressor and said "If you do anything to any of us, you will have to answer to the entire Black Community. At that juncture, we walked past him and arrived at the cafeteria, meeting applause from the many brothers and sisters who were already there.

The action was now on, as students were leaving their classes and going outside, discussing the whole situation. The brothers and sisters in the cafeteria followed our delegation outside and joined the lead of a peaceful picket line. Our revolutionary posters and placards stated our case against 400 years of legal and illegal slavery, and the deceit and hypocrisy we were facing on campus. Other posters had pictures of Malcolm X and other great African leaders.

The picket line continued to grow as more and more brothers and sisters abandoned their classes to join us. I was happy that our protest against school authorities did not become a White/Black student confrontation. We knew our strength. There was a need to watch the white students, but we targeted our appeal to the brothers and sisters.

The picket line had now grown to include up to two hundred brothers and sisters. As you know African-Americans are very creative and that is how it was on that picket line. A song developed out of nowhere. Beat Beat Bang Bang Ungowa Black Power. Beat Beat Bang Bang Ungowa BLACK POWER . The chant grew louder and lounder and still more members and other African-American students joined the picket line. Many others were involved in action designed to close down the school. Police cars began arriving and sporadic violence erupted, in what was described as a coordinated assault.

School was closed down that day and remained closed for two weeks. The Dean, 'No Neck' tried in vain to get me arrested. He claimed that I threatened him with my statement about facing the Black Community. This evil act of his was not a successful one, I suffered the consequences of my action with no regrets. Members of the Central Committee were punished, however, a stand had been taken.

Many events occurred on that day. Some students forced open the doors of the school auditorium and a short memorial for Malcolm X took place. Many brothers and sisters attended. Though our community speakers were not there, the B.S.U. Central Committee took care of the speech-making. The head counselor, a known racist, was given a serious beating by enraged students, and for once, those who walk over Black aspirations were given a taste of Black Power. I finished that semester in a continuation school.

CHAPTER 6

The Varsity

Balboa High School was quiet after political tension, however, the school and society in general, had again been warned about attempting to disregard the rights of Black people. The punishment of the rioting students was directed at the Central Committee of the B.S.U. Although the B.S.U. was eventually banned, the brothers and sisters remained together.

I was very happy to graduate from Balboa High School. It was the best way to leave the campus.

I was admitted into the University of San Francisco the following September, with a combination of luck and skills. I remained active with the movement also. The University was not one of the giant Universities, but it was a small, old private institution. The incoming Black students received a beautiful welcome from the Black students and staff, both professional and non- professional. I had made contact with one of the brothers in the B.S.U. on campus. He was a Movement brother, and he felt very happy to take me around to meet all the brothers and sisters In the University.

The freshman class had only a few Afroans, however, it was considered as having one of the highest percent. age of Blacks in the history of the University. The strict and conservative looks of the professors indicated what was in store.

The University structures and buildings portrayed the Federal money that flowed in. The five-story Library building stood out in the middle of the small campus. The Student Union building and other buildings dotted the premises.

It was great fun meeting and greeting fellow Black first-year students and very nice Afroan academic and administrative staff. Many of the newcomers were from San Francisco, however, several came from Los Angeles, Vallejo, Oakland, Berkeley, Fresno and the rest of the cities in California. Some of the Black students had similar experiences in their high schools as I did, while some were not the type that made waves.

I met and became friends with Jerry, the B.S.U. President. The B.S.U. at the University was on a much higher level than the high school trip. The game was harder to play and the stakes seemed greater. The B.S.U. leadership worked together with Afroan staff members; a cooperation that often outflanked evil conspirators. There was also a small African Students' Association on campus, which functioned as part of the International Students' Association. The A.S.A. did not meet often. I looked for, and subsequently met the President of the A.S.A. He was a Liberian - a real Liberian, not an 'American type'.

I continued my involvement in the Movement, although, the University courses and the classes therein, began to consume most of my time. Adjusting to the University was a full-time job all by itself. I was grateful to receive a lot of help from older students who tutored in-coming students.

The first year passed by quickly, with pleasure and pain. My interest in the B.S.U. activities continued. The B.S.U. carried out many of its activities in the Afroan community, and I found a way to combine my activities in the Movement in the community with those of the B.S.U.

As time went by, I found out how conservatives in the University take their racial hatred out on Afroan students. It was during my Comparative Government class that I experienced this first-hand. The lecturer stated: "1 am a veteran of World War II. I fought to defend Britain with my life. I have always admired Britain..." He went on to paint a rosy picture about how nice and sweet it was for the British to go to Africa and teach the 'natives' how to be like the British. My anger propelled me to my feet. I raised my hand as I rose from my seat. The conservative lecturer reluctantly agreed to allow my question. At the same time, I picked up a copy of Kwame Nkrumah's book, Neo-colonialism, The Last Stage of Imperialism. In a stern voice, I stated that the book I was holding contained documented proof of how much money Britain had stolen from the African Colonies. I then stated the name of the book I was holding, and before I could finish saying who the author was, I was rudely interrupted.

Here I was, for no just reason, in the middle of a dispute with a red-faced, blue-eyed, racist, conservative. He looked at me with all the disdain he could show on his old wrinkled face, and shouted in the loud paternalistic tone they always bluff us with. He said, "1 don't care what Nkrumah said. I will not have anyone in this class attempting to disgrace the name of the British. Anyone who likes can walk out right now!" Of course, he was looking right at me. I could sense that the five other Afroan students in the classroom did not like how the matter was being handled by the lecturer. At the same time, our numerical strength, 5 out of 50 students, curtailed the options. I took my seat and pounded my black fist on my desk. I realized that the classroom was his property at the moment, and I did not say any more in that class throughout the semester. I took good notes and completed the reading and written assignments, and even though I received a high grade, the lecturer remained tight-lipped any time I had time to look at his tired face.

The second year went by much faster than the first year. Towards the end of the second year, Anthony, the B.S.U. Chairman at the time, who was graduating that year, had been accepted into Law School. The B.S.U. would now need a new leadership because most of the other top members would be graduating that year.

My best friend at the University was a brother from Los Angeles. He was very well liked by the Afroan students. We sat down and put together a new program for the B.S.U. When the time came for the elections, we were the only slate with a platform and program.

Our platform called for only one Black student organization. The B.S.U. was to be renamed Pan African Students' Union. it would include the African Students' Union and the Black Students! Union. It was a noble idea to unite the Blacks, and the out-going President of A.S.A. gave his consent to the idea, and no new elections were held for his union.

The other candidates for the upcoming elections, had a considerable following and this could not be taken lightly by my friend and I. A campaign day was held so that aspirants could meet the electorate. One of the other candidates was a brother, the other, a sister. The brother was a graduate of Oakland's toughest, nearly all-Black high school, however, he was a soft- spoken and warm person. He wanted to be Chairman, but offered no program. The sister was from Los Angeles. Her speech was moving and she had good looks. Her emotional speech in the end did not offer any program. She ended by elaborating upon her desire to occupy the position.

The election results were not surprising, but very close. My slate won with a total of 37 votes, the brother, second with 25 votes, and the sister, third with 12 votes. There was no bitterness and all three of us promised to remain active members of the union.

CHAPTER 7
Jumping into the Water

My last two years in University passed by rather quickly, and the pace of my life became faster and faster. I met a Nigerian girl whom I really fell in love with at first sight! The Nigerians felt it was robbery on my part, because we stole the show. She was plump, tall and cute, and well-liked by all of the Nigerian students in the area. They felt it was all right for Nigerian men to marry Afroan sisters, but, these same people were pushed out of shape about the fact that their 'Sister' was falling in love with a 'Black American'.

The P.A.S.U. continued very strong, during my Chairmanship. The following year, the Chairmanship was held by a sister. After her year was up, my former Vice-Chairman became Chairman.

My last two years were finally over, and I was happy to be among those who made it. My direct participation in the Movement had been interrupted by my busy schedule and some personal squabbles in my organization in the community. I was no longer a member, but I remained in the Movement.

My graduation did not make me an instant success in life. I did not expect it to, however, I thought that at least, a nice job would come my way. I began my search for employment with agencies that operated throughout San Francisco. Black Program jobs were already on their way out. The feeling was that Afroan communities had been sufficiently pacified, so there was no need any longer for social programs. The Afroan communities need massive social services, but because the rebellions of the 1960's had subsided, the American mood was against any further attempts to pacify 'Niggers'.

I had exhausted personal contacts in search of a job, but to no avail. I decided to try the private sector since they were the ones hiring at the time. I knew that getting a job would be difficult, and holding it, even more difficult. I did not want to get involved with the Civil Service and the rules they have regarding participation in political activities. The private sector is no better, as it only has time for 'Niggers' who know their places. The study habits I developed during my undergraduate days helped in Graduate School. I looked for full- time jobs throughout Graduate School, but to no avail. I was hungry and my search for a job was aggressive. The many years at Patois Junior High School gave me exposure to their ways and ways of speaking.

Anyway, I was not tripping on the American dream; I was a victim of it. I was experiencing the American nightmare, called racism. I realized what was happening; the new depression was on the head of the Afroan Black man once again.

CHAPTER 8

Over. Qualified/ It Sho' is Funky

IT SHO IS FUNKY
(It Sure Is Funky)

Funk sho' is funky
Funky as a donkey
Funk sho' is funky
It sho' is funky

The party is live From wall to wall
'Til day break I'm standing tall
I know you will agree with me
It sho' is funky

If you are second-class
Fired first, hired last
Got my degree
No job for me
It sho' is funky

And Brother, if you' In
On a phony rap
A victim in a skin that's black
No way to be free
In their custody
It sho' is funky

Funk sho' is funky
It's killing you and me
Funky as a donkey
It sho' is funky

I never thought I would be considered over-qualified after completing Graduate School. My wife and I had graduated together from the same school. I applied for many jobs, however, over-qualification was the excuse offered for not employing me. How funny that most of those yelling about over-qualification, were the same ones who, a few years earlier, said that Afroans were not smart enough to attend and graduate from white universities.

I felt that inflation had pushed me to desperation. I had promised myself never to work in a Finance Company, however, I found myself in the placement office, being advised to seek employment with another Finance Company. This company was so similar to the other place where I had previously worked, in their mode of operations, that I should have known what would have happened.

I arrived at the office, dressed to kill, with a flashy gold bracelet and ring that were gifts from my wife. I entered the office and sighted two sisters, and the Assistant Manager's desk, which was located in a way that he could spy on them in particular and the movements of all the workers in general. There were no brothers in this office of ten employees.

I informed the first person I made eye contact with of my name, and of my appointment with the manager. I had finished filling out the application, when one of the girls said, "The Manager is ready to see you." I rose to my feet, taking a glance around the office. I looked at the Assistant Manager's face. He was a little bit short, and felt compelled to show a tough face to make up for the lack of stature. I could see ego was taller than his height. Some of the desks in the office had seletric typewriters but all twelve desks had green push-button telephones with about 9 extensions or lines out. The floor had a wall-to-wall carpet, which was to be expected in that type of office.

I was reminded that the manager wanted to see me by the sound of his office door being opened by the receptionist. I walked into the office and quickly sat down. As soon as I sat down, I gave the Manager a lukewarm 'hello'. I continued with an introduction, until I could see that by his facial expression, he wanted a chance to talk.

I took advantage of the fact that he wanted to talk to ease the situation. I looked at the Manager's face. It was fat and flabby. He was a monster of a man, who looked to be over 6 feet, 4 inches, with a weight of about 400 pounds. He broke the silence and said, "1 was a University football star until I broke my leg. That is why I am so big." He continued by asking me whether I played ball in the University. I gave him a firm "No." I felt insulted in a sense that many of the whites think that playing ball is the only way for a black man to make it through University. He gave me a stare, using all of his brains to figure out "What kind of Nigger is this?" The interview continued and I asked a few questions about the business, which he answered to quickly. He sat back in his swivel chair and looked at me and said, "1 am from Texas." It was a boast. "1 grew up down there and if a bunch of Southerners are talking, all I have to do is put on my boots and cowboy hat, and you could not tell me apart from any of them."

I informed him that I was born and raised in California. He checked out the application form to confirm mystory. He looked up with half a smile and said, "You lived in California all your life and did not play sports?" I finally gathered that he was a sports man, so I started running off my many past performances and glorious days of little league baseball and junior high school basketball. He suddenly warmed up, feeling he might have found a 'good Nigger'. He picked up the application and said, "Ah, I see you are married. That is a good attribute for the corporate world." All at once, he looked at the space in the form that says Wife's name. He looked up at me and said, "Your wife must be Chinese - she has a Chinese name. I felt that this was a cruel joke, and a big frown overtook my face. I responded by saying, "My wife is a Nigerian, African.

Her name is an Ibo name!" He sat back all the way to the end of the suffering swivel chair. I suddenly realized that he would not know an Ibo name from a Bini name. All at once, he slammed his feet on the floor and his body lunged forward. He said, "But I know some Nigerians; I met plenty of them in the Chicago area, but they think, well, like us, I mean, like a white man, I mean like someone with a country." He did not say anymore, but he looked at me like someone with his foot in a big metal bucket. I thought how it was people like him who kidnapped my people from Africa. The thought of the whites always trying to divide Afroans from Africans entered my mind and l understood the fear they have of all of us uniting. The reference that Nigerians are like whites, made me boil. The Manager could sense how tense his questions made the atmosphere in his office. He broke the ice by saying, "1 think I want to hire you, but you must be interviewed by my boss in Fremont. I will call you at the phone number you have given me." He gave me one final word of advice. He said, "Oh, when you go to Fremont, please don't wear any of that flash -I mean the gold bracelet on your wrist. This is a very conservative company." I left shortly after that.

I got the job, and in no time, I picked up the routine. stayed on the job long enough to see the Manager add on another brother. This would not have been possible, except that a certain number of blacks have to be hired to comply with pressure against racial discrimination.

My first day on the job, I received a verbal lashing on how the Manager did not like interracial marriages. He was surprised that I agreed with him, for my own reasons. He also warned that I was not to dip into the company's ink. That means that I was not to mess around with the white girls. That was not my bag, anyway. This type of Southerner symbolized all that old Black people had always told us young ones, about how rednecks think down south.

Time passed by quickly. The new brother hired was from New York. After four years of University sports lime light, he was back to reality. We had some things In common, and many differences, however, we preferred each other's company to that of the other people who worked in the office. The brother bought a house north of San Francisco, secretly. I, too, following family advice, and a need for a change, decided to buy a house. My house was only weeks from being approved, when the Manager said, "I just happened to run a T.R.W. credit check on you. You want to buy a house in Walnut Creek with us whites?" I informed him that the house was in San Jose, although the mortgage company handling it was in Walnut Creek. The jealousy in his eyes reminded me that he was living in a condominium, and he felt that I was moving up higher than him. He persisted, saying: "But that is a long commute and the company only wants you to live in an apartment like the one you are already in." I assured him that even though the house was located in San Jose, I would be very happy to drive to work everyday.

The following day, the manager warned me to abandon the house business, or I would lose my job. How could that be? I was only a few weeks away from my first year with the company, and I was doing well. I was fired within one week and the Manager's tears at the axing of my career, appeared to be more fake than a crocodile's.

I interviewed for another job in Palo Alto with an Insurance Company, as I definitely had to be employed before the house was approved. I explained everything to the new boss, about how I got fired from my other job, because I wanted to buy a house. He agreed to hire me, signed all of the mortgage papers, thus helping me to get the house approved. The very next day when I arrived at the office full of smiles, he shouted to his 'Southern Belle secretary saying, "Is that boy here? Send that boy into my office." I walked off the job after a heavy argument, because I knew that I was nobody's 'boy'.

CHAPTER 9

The Interview

WE ARE TOGETHER

African man
My brother, my friend
African woman
My sister, my kin

One aim, one destiny
We struggle in unity

African people
We are together
Brothers and sisters
United forever

Down with exploitation
Of our life and soul
We stand together
The young and the old

Down with our foes
Apartheid and Jim Crow
Down with colonial mentality
And that of the negro

Scattered we stand
On many a land
The black woman
The black man

African peole
We are together
Brothers and sisters
United forever

Unemployment was like a plague that everyone tries to avoid. It is difficult to avoid if you are young, gifted and Black in Jim Crow land. The dreaded disease struck and caused great suffering to me and my wife, who remained in my corner. She would oftentimes tell me that in Nigeria, education is respected, and that these people do not want to respect me.

I met hard times over the next few months; a brand new house, and no job. I checked the Want Ads everyday, chasing clown chance after chance. I remember being asked on job interviews, more than thrice, "How about that! You are a young Black with a Master's Degree; how did you manage that?" It was a rotten to think that they have a monopoly on intelligence.

One day, while searching through the scanty offerings of that day's Want Ads, I sighted a job with a company in Palo Alto, although the person to contact was to be located at a San Jose phone number. I phoned and presented myself. It did not matter that the pay would be small, as I had been out of a job for a few months. I attended the interview and was offered the job. I tried to negotiate the salary, but there was no concession.

I was given the address of the Palo Alto branch office and told to meet a Mrs. Tyler, who would also interview me and put me to work. I arrived at Palo Alto early, because I thought the San Jose /Palo Alto traffic would move slowly. Sometimes the traffic is so heavy that one moves at the speed of 5 m.p.h. I quickly located the office and bounced in to introduce myself. I was happy to start work on a professional job with steady money and career opportunities.

I was highly shocked to find that the office only had five employees, all women. I remembered the San Jose interview and my being asked whether I could work with women. This was an outrage! I sat down to a tough interview, after which she said, "Mike was right. I will hire you. All of a sudden a thought flashed through my mind as I remembered a series of interviews in Detroit, with a company that had not made a decision on whether or not to hire me. The local branch of the company thought that I was good enough for the Accelerated Training Program, so they arranged for me to fly to their Detroit home office. I had ten interviews that day in Detroit, and I decided that the ATP was a gimmick to fool the public into thinking that they are really 'making an effort to hire more Blacks in management. I remembered how excited I was after the interview in Detroit. When I touched down and contacted the local office in San Jose, I received the brush off.

My desk in this new job would be in the file room. My work was to be done in the file room. Yes, that is right; in the file room! Mrs. Tyler said that she was too busy to put me through, so, according to her, the best way for me to become familiar with the office and its operations, was to read the files as I filed them away! I told her that I did not mind reading the files, but that I could not be a file clerk. She said, "I studied for ten years to get my B.A. at night, at San Jose State University. I worked here in this office all the time." I let her know how many years it took me to get my qualifications. I also reminded her that I was a Company Representative, and not a clerk. She continued, "I am the boss here and I think reading the files is the easiest way to acquaint you with our company." I knew I would not be there for long.

That morning, I looked at the file cabinets. Each cabinet had three large drawers that rolled out at the touch of a fingertip, as if ball-bearings were at work. I looked at the lone desk at the other side of the narrow room. The weather was beautiful outside. I looked at the surrounding landscape and realized that part of Palo Alto was on the east side of the freeway, however, the poverty of East Palo Alto did not touch this eastern edge of Palo Alto. I noticed that in no time, half of the women had slipped out of the office on one errand or the other. I was not going to be turned into a file clerk, so I whiled away the time by reading the files. At lunch time, I jumped into my car to go to East Palo Alto. It was a nearly all-Black town called Nairobi by its young Blacks. Nairobi or East Palo Alto had the type of restaurant where one could buy the best barbecued beef sandwhich and the barbecued goatmeat. I could also get all of the real Soul Food I wanted. I liked the atmosphere of the place, you know, like how the brothers felt strong. That was until the San Mateo County Sheriff's Deputies arrived on the scene to force two brothers to spread eagle on their squad cars.

I started back for my office. I had a phone call to make. When I arrived at the office and parked my car, I had five minutes left in my lunch hour. I dashed to the pay phone and called the company in San Jose to ask when I would be hired. They said it would be on August 1st. I said, "Okay." I wanted to quit my job right away; but had no money. I returned to the office just in time to receive a suspicious stare. I was thirty seconds late!

When I got home that evening, my wife was overjoyed. My success in getting a job in San Jose was not the cause. She heard that 1he interviewing panel would be arriving in San Francisco to interview people interested in working in Nigeria. My wife is from Nigeria, so she was very happy that I would have the chance to work there. I was happy too. It was not that the jobs I got in the U.S.A. did not pay good salaries, but, oftentimes, my dignity as a Black man was challenged.

Things began to move very fast. As soon as completed my application, I sent it in to the Nigerian Consulate in San Francisco. About two weeks later, there was a letter in the mail stating the final date and time of the interview. The date was postponed once, but, eventually,

I found myself in the Consulate with about two-hundred other Afroans. I had a clear advantage over the other candidates. I knew all of the Consulate staff, and I had married their 'Sister'. I arrived early as most of the others did on that day. I thought would see militant revolutionary Afroans, taking their skills to the Motherland, but; I was surprised to see many elite type of Afroans. Very few of them could have been called true Pan Africanists, but all voiced a hope to be selected for the trip to Nigeria.

The Consulate with its big plush red sofas and chairs, contrasted sharply with the plush maroon carpets. The Consulate, which is very big, was overcrowded with Afroans that morning. Some of them tried to discourage me from going, so I realized that all kinds 01 Afroans were there. Watching the brothers and sisters, I was interrupted by the aroma of cakes, cookies and doughnuts that tickled my nostrils. They were not for us, but for the interviewers. Tray after tray was carried into the room where the interviewers were.

My turn for the interview had finally arrived. The interview was short and to the point. I was asked a lot of questions; some serious, some funny. I guess the funniest one was the first.

The interviewers said: "We have been trying to figure out how to pronounce your name." I cleared the confusion by telling them the one and only pronunciation. of my name. No doubt, they were wondering about how inappropriate the Afroan names are, that is, the names we received from our 'slave master'. I explained further that my friends call me Ukali, and that It is a Swahili name. I looked at the panel of interviewers. They had had a full feast on the pastries, as only empty plates and a few scattered crumbs remained on the silver serving trays. I looked directly in the face of the main interviewer. Most of the conversation started with this burly, bearded brother who, no doubt, was the leader of the panel. I had a feeling that the others had trouble understanding what I was saying, so I spoke with a confident voice, saying, "You can call me Ukali if you like." Suddenly his laughter gripped the whole room.

The interview proceeded smoothly from that point on. I felt more comfortable and so did the interviewers. They ended up the interview by telling me that I had married their 'Sister' and that meant that we were in-laws. The interview ended on a very good note. I thanked the interviewers and left. They informed me that I would be notified about their decision by mail. I left, very happy to have entered the Consulate of an African nation. I was also happy to have had an interview where my dignity as a Black man was not challenged.

CHAPTER 10

The Last Straw

I was happy that someone had arrived from the San Jose office that warm Palo Alto morning. He was In charge of the Oakland area and he said to me: "Observe operations in the Oakland area for the next couple of weeks." I was happy to exit out of that Feminist enclave where I worked. One of the women, the secretary, started filing away the files that had gathered dust. It was her job, not mine, and I was happy I did not fall for the bluff.

I quit the job eventually, and collected my salary on the last day of that month. I thought about Africa and how it would be. I also had to prepare myself for the new job I had interviewed for in Detroit, though the job was based in San Jose. My wife did not wait for the result of the Nigerian interview; she started making plans for us to return home. I thought about how I would make some nice bread on the new job; at least that was what I was told in Detroit. My thoughts on going to Nigeria, never clashed with the thought of a career with the new company.

I arrived at the new job, five minutes early, and parked my car at the rear parking lot for employees. The building had many stories and my office was on the fifth floor. It was a modern glass building that marked the landscape in that part of San Jose. I took the elevator up to the fifth floor and tightened the noose (necktie) before entering the office.

I had been in this same office nine or so weeks earlier. It was bigger than other offices I had worked in. This was one of the bigger multinationals. Its Only branch in Africa is located in South Africa. The staff was all-white, except for two Mexicans who tried to say 'hello' like 'gringos' or 'yankees'. They had learned very well how to smile and blend in. The whites all looked like the type who had grown up in a lily-white atmosphere. They looked at me to analyze whether I was a Black Militant or a good 'nigger'. There was little middle ground in their minds.

I scanned the office. The nice desks, chairs, and multi-buttoned telephones had become the regular thing in the branch offices of the multinationals. I noticed that one guy had been added to the staff since l was there last, for the initial interview. I made contact finally with Ann, who was the head of one section of the office. She was a middle-aged suburbanite, no doubt, a recent emigrant from the South. Ann led me to the Branch Manager's office after receiving the signal. I met the Branch Manager whose name was AI. He was starting to gray, and he must have agreed with Archie Bunker a hundred percent. I also met the Assistant Branch Manager who said to call him Bob. Bob was a swinger; his long black hair had the smell of expensive hair color.

The three of us had a little meeting. I received the expected time bomb. I was told that I could not just start working that day on the Accelerated Training Program that would make me an Assistant Branch Manager in eighteen months, without first of all "pr0v. ing your loyalty to the company". The look on their faces exposed their inner feelings. They did not want my rise to be so swift. We were now joined by a third middle-aged, cigarette-smoking man. He was the Representative. He gave me a plastic smile and almost immediately, joined in, "1 have been here twenty years, Larry. This is a great company."

I kicked against my not being on the A.T.P., but I knew that my next job would be in Nigeria. I thought about how my life was being played with by the forces that be. I kicked against the situation, but to no avail. The three men stuck to their guns. They felt that I should show them something. It amounted to showing them that I was a good, pliable 'nigger'. I was led by the Assistant Manager, to an empty desk. He said it was to be my desk. He then introduced me to the new, young guy. He said that the guy would be my direct supervisor, while Ann would be my overall supervisor. I Immediately asked the Assistant Manager for a few more minutes with his boss.

I felt like walking off the job. Once inside the office, I asked him if it was fair for him to have interviewed me In June, hired me in August and in the interim, interview and hire someone else whom I was to work under. I was warned not to make waves and to accept the situation and prove myself. I asked what the young man had over me. They said the same old slogan, "years and years of experience in the business." I interjected he was only a year older than I was and that he did not attend any university.

As can be expected, racial tension was in the air. All three of them became defensive. He said, "Larry, none of us has a B.A., let alone a Masters degree; but we have experience in the business. You have experience in this business too, and the best way you can show us the value of your education, is to go out there in that office and outdo that guy." I thought about how bad my financial situation was, so I told them that I would take up the challenge. In my mind, I had decided on going to Nigeria. It was the last straw.

That morning was consumed, getting familiar with my new surpervisors and office functions. At lunch, I dialed my wife at work, and she said that she was just about to phone me. She said that the Consulate had informed her that we had received appointments in Nigeria. We celebrated on the phone, until, the looks of the other office workers with frowning faces, told me that I had laughed too loud.

I continued with the phone conversation on a pay phone, so that I could discuss in privacy. My wife continued, "They are going to pay our fares to Nigeria, along with allowances, and you don't have to worry about your dignity as a Black man being insulted anymore. In Nigeria, everyone is black." I wanted to leave right away, but I knew there would have to be plans and preparations.

I continued with my job until a freaky motor accident put me out of action. The people at the office could not figure out where I was coming from, and so questions remained unanswered. I continued my preparations from my sick bed. My back became more of a nagging pain, more than anything else.

The day I became convinced that my back was not responding to Western medicine, I pulled my painful body out of bed, and traveled with my wife to the Consulate for an exit interview with the Consul-General. He gave us our tickets and a partially filled out contract. He said that the contract would be completed as soon as we arrive in Nigeria. A telegram stating our intended arrival was being prepared.

My family held a beautiful send-off party and I threw another to boot. On a cold winter night in San Francisco, my wife and I were accompanied by some members of my family and some of our friends, to the International Airport. Some members of my family could not go to the airport because it would have been too rough on them to experience my departure. In our rush to hand in our luggage, I burst my fingernail, with all of the impact of a falling metal trunk. My back seized the opportunity to hurt like hell. My momentum carried me until it was announced that we were in the air, headed for New York.

We arrived in New York the next morning, and took a taxi to our good Nigerian friend, Billy's house in Brooklyn, not too far from the airport. New York looked very old compared to California. We arrived at Billy's apartment, and had a nice shower. Later, his Mississippi-born, beautiful Afroan wife, arrived from her lob, but she had to return to work. Billy was off because of a terrible accident suffered the day before. His car was completely destroyed the day before we arrived. So Billy was happy to be alive.

He phoned one of his good Nigerian friends, who arrived and took us out for a day on the town. We were careful to take care of the business we had to do while enjoying New York. We visited up to five Nigerians, and had as much to drink as we could hold. All of the brothers and sisters we had visited, wished us a safe journey.

It was, all of a sudden, time to be at the airport enroute to Nigeria. We did what was necessary to make the weighing of our loads quicker. As we were ready to board the flight, Billy took one last look at me and said his last words to me before our departure. He looked at me up and down, and said, "If you are a strong, tough, Black man, you will make it in Nigeria, however, if you think you are making an easy trip, then you will fail." The last call was made for us to board the jet, and we quickly said 'bye' to Billy. We were on the jet headed for Africa.

CHAPTER 11

The Great Leap over the Pond

ON AFRICAN LAND

On African land
On green foliage hills
and fertile plateaus
and dusty dirt roads

And the cultural setting
Of the old and new
Cross a river in a canoe
With an African crew

From the tropical south
To the flat plains of Nigeria's north
View Benin's art
Watch a traffic jam start

And those tall African trees
And a people off their knees
Life in a Black country
Is really something to see

You can arrive by air
And see a taxi there
A taste of life
With all the spice

The Black woman is queen
On the African sceen
Home of the Black Man
On African LAND

It was a cold, windy, rainy, winter afternoon. The dark of night was approaching as we fastened our seat belts. The airport was jumping with activity, even as the big jet lifted its heavy frame and pointed its nose upward, heading east. Once the jet reached a certain height, the engines were turned down, and the cabin was level once again.

I looked at my fingernail that was still burst. The whole fingernail was covered with dried up blood and bits of damaged nail. I thought about how all journeys leave their mark, one way or the other. My finger looked terrible, but the throbbing pain had subsided into a nagging type of pain. I pushed the pain out of my mind, thinking about how things would be when we touch down.

I had read as many books about Africa, discussed Africa with so many Africans and Afroans who had been there, that one would think I knew it all about Africa. As the jet continued on its way to Africa, I suddenly had two- thousand more questions to ask about Africa. I continued waking up my wife from her sleep, to ask her more about the motherland. She understood my excitement but begged me to try and sleep because I would need a good night's sleep to arrive, looking well. I had many more questions, but I decided to let the events of the next few days answer them.

All night, the jet continued flying. We could only see the Atlantic Ocean below. I woke up from knocking my tender fingernail against my knee. I opened my eyes and ears to the noise of one certain group of passengers. I suddenly realized that majority of the passengers were white, on this African- bound jet. I thought about how jet fares to Africa were higher than fares to Europe, and yet the distance is nearly the same. So the high fares, would definitely keep Afroans from traveling to Africa -- home.

All at once, mass laughter broke out as the group I had noticed earlier started jumping up and down, acting like kindergarten children. They were all American whites. I wondered what kind of group it was, and where their destination was.

I managed the taste of the campact breakfast that was served and an added extra cold drink. I started once again, thinking about how Africa would be. I knew that one thing for sure was that the people I would see, would all. be black. My thoughts were again interrupted by hysterical and immature laughter of the wild group. I looked at them to see if they were a bunch of hippies. Although some of the males had long hair, the wild stringy beards were absent. I looked at their faces again and deduced immediately, if not mistakenly that they were a group of university freshmen or sophomores, on some type of tour. They were making more noise by this time and my wife said that they must be Peace Corps members, going to Africa.

I looked at them again and by this time, they were in the seats on the opposite side of the aisle. It seemed as though two or three of them would visit each group of seats, encouraging the others within the group. I was very disturbed, 'You mean African countries still trust the Peace Corps in Africa?' My wife said that Africa did have quite a way to go if they still trust them. I asked her how that group could do anything, other than cause disorder, because their ages ranged from 18 to 21, though a few of them were a little older.

The announcement from the pilot was the only thing that brought the noise to a halt. The announcement said we would soon touch down in Monrovia, Liberia. The time was almost at hand, when I would have the feeling of actually standing on African land.

My wife nudged me and said "I heard one of them say they were going to Kenya." I was happy that we did not have the same destination.

The jet began its descent for the tiny airport in Liberia. In no time at all, the doors of the plane were opened, and stairs were pushed up to the jet. We were informed that we could stay in the airport lounge until it was time to take off. Some of the passengers had reached their destination, and had now entered the Customs line.

We were among the last people off the jet. That wild group was at the beginning of the line. Finally, we made our way to the door. I walked out of the door before my wife, and I was greeted by a slap from the hot steamy weather. It was a clear day in Monrovia, and I had the feeling that since I was elevated, I could see for miles in any direction. The air was humid and the airport was surrounded by trees.

We started walking towards the little lounge, where we could sit down and have a nice cold drink. The building was dingy. The air inside was as warm as the air outside.

We had finished our drinks and had started ordering seconds, when the little speaker on the wall, blared out a message. It was time to board our jet, which would be bound for Nigeria. I had no trouble finishing my drink because the heat made me thirsty. My vest and jacket were being carried under my arm, because there was no need for them in all that heat.

We boarded the jet after the rush for the door. As I made my way up the metal stairs, I glanced at the workers who were unloading some of the baggage. I, all of a sudden, started walking slowly, because I wanted to make sure that my suitcases were not among those being unloaded. The pushing and shoving b~ those behind us, would not really allow our slow paceI ! however, before we reached the cabin, I was sure n0n, of our luggage was among those being carted away. There was a short delay on the ground, after which we were in the air again.

As soon as the jet reached a certain height, the cabin was once again level. The wild laughter from the immature group started all over again. Other passengers on the jet continued to heap ugly stares al this wild group. The group continued as if they were the only people on the jet.

The sky was clear as the morning sun lit up the sky. In no time at all, it was noon and we were touching down. The hot, humid weather gave me another welcome slap as we stepped down the mobile metal stairs. We were confined to the transit lounge, although this airport seemed a little bigger than the other one. We were now in the Ivory Coast.

Once inside, the fans worked to provide a good flow of air. In this airport, everyone seemed to be speaking French. We were looking at the various displays in display cases, when we were greeted in English by one of the salesmen. The loud speaker carried a message that it was time for passengers to board the jet. In a few minutes, we were in the air, headed for Nigeria.

CHAPTER 12

To Enter Lagos

The jet was in the air, long enough to level out and provide for us a view of the beautiful West African landscape. The noisy group continued their hysteria, as though for many of them, this was their first time of being beyond parental custody. They confirmed my belief that Africans were getting a mixed bag of nuts in that bunch. When the announcement was made that we were nearing the airport, where we were to land, I felt a sense of relief.

It took about twenty minutes after touching down, before the metal stairway was put into place for us to alight. The cabin doors were open, and I jumped to my feet, happy to get away from the wild group. I grabbed the carry-on luggage, while putting on my suit coat. My wife was also making sure she gathered her handbag and other things. We felt ready to meet the people who should have been notified about our eminent arrival. It was a late Friday afternoon.

I stood at the cabin door, and took a long, deep breath of Nigerian air. My turn had arrived to exit the jet. I wanted to be sure not to fall down the stairs like a former clumsy U.S. President. There would be no aides to cushion my fall. I started down the stairs with my wife, slowly at first, and with more confidence, as I touched the ground. I thought about how some Afroans kiss the ground when they first land in Africa. I must have been tripping in a world of my own, when my woman, who was by my side, nudged me, and reminded me that we had to report to the baggage-claim area. We arrived there just in time to see two trucks, each carrying some of our suitcases to the baggage-claim area.

We claimed our baggage, after a little wait and were on our way to the Customs, when we ran into a group of dividers, where our visas and medical certificates were checked.

The Customs were next, and there stood two tall Nigerians, fully dressed in their uniforms, standing at attention in a strict manner. Both of them had small batons and stern looks on their faces. They began picking through our luggage, as though they were looking through a department store catalogue.

My face was as wet as a wet towel, because, sweat began to pour out through all the pores of my body. My clothes were best suited for the cold I had left in San Francisco, and the winter I had met in New York. I noticed ceiling fans that were turned up to the highest speed, yet, sweat continued to pour down my face. I could see all of my luggage and the anxious group of touts and taxi drivers with big smiles on their faces, as we passed through the final phase of the Customs exercise.

I could hear them saying, "American man, give us dollars." I looked at them and wondered how they knew that I was an Afro-American, and not a Nigerian. Afterall, all the Nigerians are black like me. Many wear the best three-piece suits, made anywhere in the world. The fact that my wife is a Nigerian, somehow, helped to make Customs easier to bear. I felt less of a man at first, because she was doing all the talking, but if I had interfered, it would not have brought about desired results.

My wife continued to speak in her language and in broken English to the Customs officials. She used her knowledge of and understanding of Yoruba, also, before we were waved on by the Customs officials. We were now cleared and ready to declare our cash assets. Again, this important task, had to be carried out by my wife. I was not new to Nigerians, though, because there were many I knew in San Francisco. I was only new to the Nigerian ways.

While my wife, who felt completely at home and at ease, was led to the place where money is declared, I stayed behind to keep my eyes on our luggage. I was joined by about twenty-five touts and taxi drivers. I knew that if my eyes wandered, my luggage would disappear. I looked at the brothers and noticed that the average height seemed to be 5 feet, 6 inches. I forgot that everyone was not that short, but for the moment, I felt like a tall brother. A circle formed around me and my luggage, while I kept my eyes on every single piece of luggage continuously. Some of the touts and taxi drivers were, no doubt, arguing who would get the big fish; me as a passenger. My face was as wet as one who had dipped his head in a bucket of water.

My wife appeared back on the scene, with a smile on her face. She felt so much at ease, that I knew everything would be okay. There was no trace of any government official to welcome us, as we had been assured of in the Consulate, back in San Francisco. We moved our luggage to the sidewalk just outside the main door to the airport. We had to discuss what our next move would be, of course with our eyes on our luggage.

Lagos was full of activity; an International Trade Fair was on. All major hotels were commandeered by the government for people invited to the Trade Fair. This was the advice we were given as we sat in the back of one of the two vehicles we had chartered to carry our luggage.

Lagos is a combination of modern urban development and urban decay. Actually, we were in Ikeja, which is a few miles out of what is called Lagos or Eko. We were on our way to Airport Hotel which is very nice, only to arrive and find out that there was no vacancy.

I could read tension on the faces of the taxi drivers. They wanted their money so they could go, unless we would pay more for their efforts in helping us to locate a vacant hotel. We tried two more decent hotels, only to find that they, too, were fully booked. My wife, at this point, said that we should look for her cousin. She had the address, but I told her that we had to stop and release the taxi drivers, before ideas became plans and then realities.

I looked up and from a distance, I could see what looked like a decent hotel ahead. When I told the driver to pull into that hotel, I noticed that we were on one of Ikeja's busy streets. People were all over the place. The two record shops who were competing for the ears of the public, had their loudest volume buttons on.. The sounds were mainly Reggae and Soul music. I noticed that there was a definite trend in the music; it was the deejay type of Reggae - I Roy, U Roy, Dillinger, Peter Tosh and Bob Marley.

We were now entering the driveway to Hotel Grandeur International. I felt that at least our baggage should be secure. I felt like I was in a giant Black ghetto. All of a sudden, everyone was Black; the drivers, the guard at the hotel, the Owner/Manager of the hotel, and every police and soldier. One could see a few whites, however, they moved around quietly and unceremoniously, thereby becoming insignificant. Africa overshadows every other element within it, with the black skins of millions of Africans.

I met the madam who owned the hotel, and asked her for a large room. She showed us what she had. My wife and I agreed that I should stay behind with our baggage, while she went to look for her cousin. All of the workers in the meantime, made sure to tell us that the drivers were overcharging us. Anyway, they all helped to take our luggage to our room, which was all there in no time. Sweat continued to pour down my face, non-stop, although I lifted very little. I was happy when my wife nudged me and said, "Tip them." I paid the drivers who put up a big fuss because greed had overtaken their emotions and common sense.

I locked my room with the key I had been given, and I escorted my wife out to the street and hailed a taxi, which she left in to find her cousin. She was well on her way down the busy street. I unlocked my door, using that type of key for the first time, I had noticed. I counted my baggage and was happy they were all there.

My next thought was to seek relief from the heat because the room was like an oven. I opened the window, only to hear my neighbor taking care of business with some chick. I did not want to be a witness, so I pulled the long sliding glass door to where only my room was exposed enough to allow for air. I noticed that there was a ceiling fan, and I figured out how to turn it on. The air was starting to flow when I decided to look closely at the wall plugs. They were different from any ones I had ever seen. Sweat continued to bother me, so I grabbed a suitcase so that I could pull out a pair of jeans and an 'airconditioned' undershirt.

Once I found the clothes, I turned towards the window, took in some of Africa's air and started removing my coat. I forgot that I was under a ceiling fan. I felt the breeze that was being created by the blades of the fan, coming so close to my hands, as I was attempting to change. Suddenly, I noticed what was happening and moved my hands away quickly. It was my first encounter with a ceiling fan. I sat down on the thin mattress that was supported by a weak frame and pulled off my coat and vest. Meanwhile, a thought entered my mind - I had entered Lagos!

CHAPTER 13

To the North

We stayed in Lagos for about five days, as there were many things to do.

My wife arrived at the hotel with her cousin, Theresa, and a van. We loaded our luggage on to the van and moved them to a safer place in Ikeja. Theresa offered us her bed in the traditional type of African hospitality. I was so happy that we received such a warm reception, including nice egwusi soup and eba for dinner. We were anxious not to impose ourselves, espcially in view of the fact that she was not expecting us. I felt that as employee's of the government, it would be best for my wife and I to lodge in a hotel so that our expenses could be documented properly.

We found one manageable place, not too far from my wife's cousin's house. It was general knowledge that all of the better hotels had their available rooms commandeered by the government, as the Lagos International Trade Fair was on. The very first night in the little hotel, I found out that although our room had an airconditioner, the bedbugs had a feast on our legs.

The second night, Theresa's neighbor, whose name was Abu, was standing outside of this house watching as I passed by on my own way. He, like all the other people around, had heard that there was an Afroan around. He came up to me and introduced himself to me, I did the same, and we shook hands. In no time, we became friendly and both of us asked each other many questions about our different backgrounds. Abu looked like any other brother from San Francisco to New York. Later on he said, "1 would like to take you out for a drink a little bit later." I continued on to the hotel, and there, I told my wife about my new friend. Chinwe, my wife asked me to describe the person, which I did. She said that she had noticed him looking at us when we had first arrived at her cousin's house. She continued, "He might be a nice guy, but we should ask Theresa about him, because she would know what kind of person he is." In the meantime, we were informed that dinner was being served in the hotel. When we saw the food and the atmosphere, we were glad we had Theresa's house to eat at. When we arrived at her house, I told her about Abu, and she said that he was cool.

That night, I went out with Abu in his car, and we drove to Airport Hotel. While we were on the way, he brought out a Nigerian brand of cigarette, and we smoked while we were driving along lively Isheri Road, until we reached our destination.

The music has heavy, once we were seated in the garden. Abu ordered a beer for me and begged the bar man to give him one cold beer for his friend from America. The bar man said, "Only warm one remain." Abu continued to beg the bar man to find one cold beer for his friend. I interrupted by saying, "Abu, if you can drink it warm, then I can too." It was obvious that the bar man did not have any cold beer. I was told that there had been a power blackout for the last two hours. I enjoyed my bottle of Harp with Abu and some other brothers, who were friends of Abu. Abu refused to let me pay for my beer, and demanded that I take another. He was just about to call the bar man when I told him that I probably could not finish even one bottle, because I had noticed that the Nigerian beer bottles were twice as big as the bottles I was used to.

The night life was heavy, and the high fashioned girls reminded me of urban Afroan girls. Abu hinted to me that those were the expensive girls of Nigeria. We finished our beer, and Abu took me back. On the way back, he asked me whether any of the 'American

Negroes' had tribal marks. I corrected him on our correct identity, letting him know that we were not known as 'Negroes' anymore. I went on further to explain to him that all African customs were banned during slavery, therefore, we did not have any tribal marks.

On Monday, my wife and I got up early, because we had so many things to do. We reported to the Federal Public Service Commission in Lagos, of our arrival to the country, and asked if the telegram sent by the Consul General in San Francisco had been received. They said that they had not received any telegram, otherwise, they would have sent a special bus to pick us up from the airport. They also said that they would have got us settled in a proper hotel, until we knew where we would be posted. At that moment, the officer who was assisting us, asked us to look out of the window. He said, "It is going to pick up people arriving today", as he pointed at an official bus. We happened to be looking out from the seventh floor of the giant twenty-five storied Independence Building.

We asked that we be posted to the Northern State of our choice. The officers responsible for posting, said that it would be all right with them if we wanted to be posted to the North, however, they advised us that it might work out better for us if we chose a Southern state like my wife's home state. My wife stated her reasons for wanting to go up North, and they reluctantly agreed. We were then referred to the State's Liaison Office in Lagos.

After a cool reception at the State Liaison Office, we were given air tickets to that state. Early the following morning, we were in the airport ready to board the jet. We left most of our baggage in my wife's cousin's house, to be picked up at a later date.

We arrived in Kaduna, after a long flight over the Nigerian countryside. The airport was not in the middle of urban sprawl, but located some distance away from the main town. The Liaison Officer in Lagos had told us that we would be met at the airport by officials from the Ministry of Education. We looked in vain for the people upon our arrival.

Since we did not see any of the government officials, we took a taxi straight to the Ministry we had been assigned to. The ride was very interesting. The long, wide streets here, contrasted the ever expanding go-slow of the coast. The city was very clean, again a complete contrast to the coast. Then I remembered being told, before leaving the coast, that up country is like a different country. The moderate climate contrasted the hot, steamy weather of the south, and instead of a go-slow, the traffic was moving swiftly down Ahmadu Bello Way, until we turned near Durbar Hotel, which was built during FESTAC. We passed a huge building called Luggard Hall.

We finally arrived at the Ministry of Education, which was a long two-storied building. After unloading our luggage from the taxi, and stacking them in a neat pile, I asked my wife if it would not be risky to leave them out in the open, while we go into the offices. She assured me that our things would be safe. She continued, "This is the North. The people are Moslems. They don't steal like in the South." I knew that the people were Moslems, but my experience in the airport in Lagos, made me vigilant.

We left our suitcases and I carried only my briefcase. Once inside, we asked around for information, only to find out that it was best if we understood the language of the area, because many of the people choose or do not want to speak 'Turunchi' or English. Finally, we found the office of the Chief Inspector of Education and reported our situation. We were taken to the Passages Office of the Ministry, where our accommodation would be taken care of. As we arrived at the Passages Office with the messengers that accompanied us, I looked over the aisle at our baggage, downstairs. The suitcases were all there, unmolested, so I was happy as we entered the Passages Office.

Once inside, we were told that we would be taken to Tourist Lodge, even though, we found out later that most expatriates were taken to Durbar or Hamdala Hotel; the two international hotels in Kaduna. A driver was given the task of driving us to Tourist Lodge. We were given a letter to present to the management of the hotel and asked to report back to the Ministry the following day after we were situated.

The Tourist Lodge was not far from the Ministry. Our driver had a Landrover vehicle and sped towards our destination. I noticed Durbar Hotel, as we rolled toward the street that leads to Tourist Lodge. We turned into a driveway that led to the parking lot. We parked and presented our letter to the receptionist, who was a lady of Nigerian and Ghanaian parentage. The driver remained outside.

Some guys who worked for the hotel, helped us to carry our suitcases to our room. Our room was on the second floor, right on top of the bar. I tipped the guys that helped us and also thanked them. The room was small, but it had a self-contained bathroom and an air conditioner. We could manage it, because we figured we would not be there long, anyway. After taking a little time to arrange our things, we went downstairs to have our dinner.

We ate dinner in a hurry because of the journey we had to make to Zaria that night. I knew my wife was in a hurry to see her parents who live there, so I finished my nice rice and chicken stew quickly. As soon as we finished our dinner, the waiter brought a receipt for me and said that I should sign it. I signed it and also asked for directions to the Zaria motor park.

We were now on the streets of Kaduna, looking for a taxi to take us to the motor park. It was to cost 60 kobo for the two of us, so we entered the back door of the Peugeot 504. The taxi driver was a Southerner, who seemed well at home in the North.

When we arrived at the motor park, all one could see were cars. All were taxis and some of them had their destinations painted on the body and rear wind shields. Some of them read KanolZaria. A few were going to Lagos. In addition to the taxis which charged the highest rates in the motor park, were vans and mini-buses. The brothers had an orderly system, and in no time, we were in the back seat of a Peugeot 504 station-wagon taxi, which we chartered for-N-10 (ten naira).

After riding through the vast empty countryside, we arrived at our destination, Zaria. The road was a very good two-laned highway. After an hour, we arrived at the doorsteps of my wife's father's house. Her baby sister was the first to begin shouting in excitement at seeing us, and in no time, all of her brothers and sisters and, of course, the parents, came out to hug us.

That was a beautiful time to meet my in-laws for the first time in person. We related our experiences, so far in the country, and went to bed.

The next day, we left for Kaduna in one of my in-laws cars, and reported back to the Chief Inspector of Education. An argument ensued, between us and the clerk in the C.I.E.'s office because of a language problem. He did not understand my intonation, and he covered up by saying, "These Americans are pushing me around." I thought the incident was minor, but the C.I.E. had a great frown when we were eventually allowed to see him.

I remembered that I did not have my transcripts, but, I did have my certificates. The C.I.E. explained that he would need the transcripts in order for him to post me to a proper place. I told him that I have all my certificates with me, and the Consulate in San Francisco had all of my transcripts and had verified my certificates before I even got to Nigeria. The C.I.E. refused to consider a list of my courses listed in my resume and refused to post us until our transcripts were produced. We sent letters and telegrams back to the United States to get copies of our transcripts, but there was no reply for at least three weeks. In the meantime, we reported to the Ministry nearly everyday. I finally realized that our transcripts had been packed among our books that would be arriving by sea a few months later. We explained this to the C.I.E., but he remained adamant, keeping us in limbo.

Since the C.I.E. was playing with our lives, we decided to apply to the big Polytechnic, a post-secondary technical institution, in Kaduna. It took about four weeks before we finally received letters of appointment, even though we were interviewed in the meantime. We were appointed as Lecturers in the Polytechnic.

A dispute broke out between us and the authorities over housing. I was informed that we would not be housed, even though it was a policy for them to house expatriates. I was also told that I would not be given contract benefits. I tried to make a case for myself, because, I knew, after hours of searching, that it was almost impossible to find good accommodations in the beautiful, but crowded capital. My in-laws said that we could live with them fifty miles away and commute everyday until the matter was settled, but my pride would not let me consider that option.

In the meantime, we went back to Lagos and got new appointment letters from the Commission, who posted us to a Southern state. I chose the place I wanted to go to, which was the only Southern state in need of teachers. We traveled back to the North to see how the chips would fall.

When we returned, we found out that the C.I.E., was also the Chairman of the Board of Governors of the Polytechnic, and that he had found out about our employment with the Polytechnic. He had also started making arrangements to have our letters of appointment withdrawn. His stand on transcripts was not upheld by the higher institution, even though the C.I.E. could only post us to secondary schools. In the meantime, the Ministry cut off the payment on our hotel room.

Naturally, we felt that our new employer would provide housing in the staff housing, or in the guest house owned by the Polytechnic, across the bridge in Kakuri, until housing was eventually provided. Instead, the Director and the white Housing Officer told us to move into a guest house in Tudun Wada because the other guest house which was located in the southern part of Kaduna was being held over for a Mr. Dale - a white expatriate, who had been in the Durbar Hotel for ten days! At this point, I made a case, "Why not put us in Durbar until accommodation is located?" This proposition was rejected, and that meant that we were bound to stay in the dusty Tudun Wada guest house.

Our dispute with the Director of the institution turned into an open conflict, and the argument ended up with him saying he would call the Commissioner of Police to have me deported, He would not let me talk and when he said, "Don't talk", I blew my top. We walked off the job.

In the meantime, a well-meaning friend advised me to take the issue to the American Consul for clarification.

I refused, for the fact that I did not want to bring whites into a Black-on- Black squabble. This well-meaning individual, however, made a trip to the American Consulate and discussed the issue with the Consul, who I found out laughed throughout. The Consul advised the well-meaning individual that he should "Allow the Black American to find his roots." How cynical it was of him; that was why I did not even want to go to the American Consulate in the first place, because I knew I did not need their help for any problem I encountered in Africa. My mind now was made up--I was headed for Bendel State where we had been reposted to in Lagos, to see what life there would show me.

Larry Ukali Johnson-Redd

LAGOS REMEMBERED

It is ugly and pretty
It was the capital city
And like New York City
Not very much pity

Full of historic places and
Walls of Black faces
And the Oba's palaces
With cultural traces

Hear Afro beat
And reggae tunes
And sweet soul music
If you choose it.

On the bridges
or the freeway
Have a good time
Every day.

Nightlife and skycrapers
The music will boom
And there is a hot sun
In the afternoon.

You can eat
Or you can dine
And the sisters
Are really fine

On Lagos Islands
And many lagoons
Enjoy the beaches
And the sound of the tunes.

CHAPTER 14

Arrival at the Crossroads

BENIN ARRIVAL

It was a rainy
Tropical African night
We made Benin
On the last evening flight

Something on
A golf tournament
Hotel rooms commandeered
By the Government

This was my arrival
In Bendel
We spent the first night
At Central Hotel

We tried to take a Bendel Line bus straight to Benin City, through Ibadan, but the bus was full of people who had entered in Kano. There were only a few seats left on the bus for people boarding in Zaria. The passengers waiting in Zaria were more than the few seats left on the bus, so we did not have any chance of getting on. The following day, I was determined to go. The bus arrived from Kano, full of people; some sitting in the aisle. I was so angry, that I got into an argument with the Bendel Line staff. In a move of desparation, we sped off towards Kaduna, which had the nearest airport. The ride was comfortable in my parent-in-law's car. My in-laws tried so hard to get us situated in the North, that the feeling of guilt for leaving, occupied one corner of my mind as we entered the airport. My wife's folks bade us farewell.

We were very lucky, because since we had no reservations, we were on a jet bound for Lagos, within an hour. Once in Lagos, we made a trip to the Bendel State Liaison Office. Accommodation was no problem for us this time. There was no trade fair on, so we stayed at the Airport Hotel in Ikeja.

The Liaison Officer was a very nice Bendelite and the Reggae on his small cassette let me know that he was not a square. He greeted us very well and asked me if I was enjoying the country. I told him that I had to be settled first. He agreed with that, He looked my woman in the eye and said, "So you have brought a brother home to us. This is beautiful." I was touched.

I told the Liaison Officer that I wanted to report to Bendel as soon as possible. He felt my sense of urgency and said, "Okay, where are you staying now?" We informed him and he said that he would send a driver with our air tickets later that afternoon. I was impressed by his business manners, friendliness and general attitude. It was early afternoon, so we took a taxi to the Federal Palace Hotel to have lunch.

The Federal Palace Hotel is definitely an international class hotel. A new addition was being added, we could see, as we drove up the round-about. We discharged the taxi driver, whom we had overpaid. We entered the lobby and were directed to the restaurant. We took our seats and were happy that we would be going to Bendel State later that day; a place I had never visited before. We waited and waited, thinking that one of the waiters would come over to our table. Meanwhile, a white couple entered and took their seats very close to our table. Within a second, two workers were there to attend to them. I was outraged, jumped to my feet and I said, "1 have been in the white man's land where they have preference for the whites, but I am not going to see that nonsense here in Africa!" The worker probably did not understand every word I said, but when I took the matter to the management, I received a half- hearted apology. We had our lunch, eventually, while we took in the view of the lagoon, before jumping into a taxi back to our hotel.

When we arrived, our tickets were waiting, so we packed quickly, and were on our way to the airport. It was 5:00 p.m. when we arrived at the airport, just in time to catch the last flight to Benin City, Bendel State. We were on that jet as it lifted off the runway in the midst of the tropical darkness that was fast approaching.

The flight from Lagos to Benin is a very short flight. We were glad to be on our way to a better situation. The small jet soared over the thick bush below. We could see the many farms among the rubber and palm trees. In less than thirty minutes, we were approaching the BenIn City Airport. The darkness of night raced with our small skypower jet, for a place on the runway.

The jet stopped after a smooth touchdown. The metal stairwell was put into place and passengers began to alight from the aircraft. One airport bus was waiting on the tarmac to take the passengers to the airport terminal building. We collected our baggage at the terminal and were met by up to eight taxi drivers. All of them wanted the business of conveying us to our place of destination. In the meantime, we asked airport officials about decent hotels, only to be informed that all major hotels had been booked up due to a golf tournament going on in the city, however, we were advised to go to Central Hotel on Akpakpava Street.

The taxi driver was very cheerful and he helped us carry our luggage to his taxi. We drove out of the airport, taking a left turn on Airport Road, until we got to Ring Road. On Ring Road, I noticed a circular park in the middle of the famous city round-about. I also saw a round building which I later found out was a museum. The great circular building stood among other smaller buildings and green grass in the ring, as we sped around the circular thoroughfare into the smooth exit onto Akpakpava Road.

We continued down Akpakpava, a very lively street. It reminded me of the main drag of any Black community. We entered the driveway for Central Hotel and the management confirmed that a suite was available. The driver and I unloaded our luggage from the taxi, and workers from the hotel carried them up to our room.

The room was large with an air conditioner, but there was a power blackout. In the meantime, one of the workers brought us candles. The blackout was over in an hour, and the heat that had overtaken the room began to disappear with the air conditioner now on.

My wife and I decided to go and buy insect spray among other things we needed. We locked our room and walked down the stairs, towards the walkway that led to the street. We had just made our way into the street when I noticed a procession heading down the street. I had always thought that I knew a lot about Africa, but I surely did not know what type of procession it was. As the procession drew closer and closer to us, the drumming and chanting became louder and louder. I swallowed my ego and asked my wife what was going on. She told me that it was a funeral procession.

The next morning, after a cold water bucket bath, we reported to the Public Service Commission. The hotel staff had given us directions and we entered a taxi headed towards Ring Road. The taxi driver pushed his way into the traffic and soon, we were moving down Sapele Road, towards the group of buildings that houses the Public Service Commission. We reported to the Secretary, a handsome and intelligent administrator. He gave us a nice and warm welcome and arranged for transportation to take us to the Ministry of Education and the State Board of Education. We thanked him sincerely.

When we arrived at the Ministry, my wife reported for her posting. At the State Board of Education, I received my posting to a local secondary school. The gentlemen we reported to there, gave us a nice welcome, even though the first person we met looked at us as though he had a problem smiling. I did not expect everyone to like me, but feelings did not have to be displayed so openly in a professional setting.

I was posted to a local secondary school as a Lecturer to introduce Government as a subject in that school. The school was located in the historic Benin City, capital of Bendel state.

Bendel State is truly the crossroads of Nigeria because all of the major ethnic and religious groups are represented In one way or the other. The Ibos are in Bendel State, Yoruba is spoken in the northwest, while Edo is spoken in Benin The Etsako's include many Islamic people. There are the Ishan and Ora people. I was once informed that the name Bendel was derived from Benin and the Delta area. The Delta area includes the Ijaws, Itshekiri's, Urhobo's and the Etsoko's. Bendel is the crossroads or junction of integration in a giant Black Nation.

IN SWEET BENIN

On the scene
in sweet Benin
You can see
Almost anything

On the scene
In sweet Benin
See the people
Doing their thing

In the market
The women sell and buy
In the bars
Some men drink

In the offices
Some people are cheating
But you better know
The people are seeing
And seeing is beleiving

On the scene
In sweet Benin
The Black Man is King
And Black Woman is queen

An 'live' is the night scene
The people dance and the people sing
Disco houses throughout Benin
Come on baby let's do our thing

On the streets of Benin
Eat barbecue called suya
See our culture sing
Check out the scene in sweet Benin

CHAPTER 15

Getting Down in Benin

What does it mean to get settled in Benin? In order to change over, an Afroan has to observe how things are done.

We asked that we be taken to a better hotel; we wanted to go to Hotel Plaza or Emotan, but one can not get all that one desires, every time. However, we were told by the State Board that we could get better accommodation at a place that the Board had had a previous agreement with, because the hotel in which we had already checked into did not have any credit agreement with the Board.

The second day of our arrival in Benin, we checked out of Central Hotel and when our suitcases were all brought out, the officer in the Board, who was to take us to the new hotel, refused to allow any of our suitcases in his car. So we hailed a taxi and followed the officer to the new hotel. The new hotel was called Crown Hotel. It was a nice hotel by Nigerian standards.

I was still hooked on taking hot baths, so the following morning I asked the workers where I could get hot water, since there was no running hot water, except cold water in the bathroom. The hotel workers assured me that we would have hot water whenever we wanted it. I took them up on it and in thirty minutes, there was a knock on the door and a bucket of boiling hot water.

I reported to the school I had been posted to, the following day. I met my Principal. He was a stately African gentleman. He had the height and physique that demanded respect. I told him that we had to have a house, or at least a better hotel, because I had it In my mind that we would be put up in one of the top two hotels in town. This never happened. He joked, "You are as black as I am."

The Bursar of the school accompanied me by taxi back to the hotel. My wife was there and I introduced the Bursar to her and explained that we would be going to a better hotel. In the meantime, I ordered a beer from the bar for the Bursar. We quickly packed our luggage and though I knew that I would not be going to one of the top two, I was more anxious to eat my wife's egwusi soup in our own place.

We accompanied the Bursar to the Edo Guest House. This place was different from the other places, because it had a group of chalets. There was a period of tense negotiations between the Bursar and the hotel manager, after which hotel workers took our luggage to one of the chalets.

The chalet had a sitting room with many chairs and a powerful ceiling fan. The bedroom had an air conditioner and two twin beds pushed together to make a king size bed, and a walk-in bathroom. There was also a desk in the sitting room. The Iouvred windows had screens or gauzes. This hotel was by no means one of the top two, however, we managed to make ourselves comfortable for what we thought would be a short stay there.

I sat down in the sitting room after the Bursar had left and thought about how amazed the Principal was at my shade of black. I also thought about how many misguided Afroans felt that all Africans are very dark. I gathered from what the Principal said, that in Africa most people think that all Afroans are from light to almost white in complexion, There was no doubt in my mind that all Blacks need better communication in order to learn about each other.

I left for school early that morning, hoping that I could get settled as soon as possible. The distance from the hotel seemed like an endless journey. In fact, both of us left in different directions trying to get over in a fast-moving world. The New Lagos Road go-slow was at its best, allowing my sweat a chance to soak my body. I wiped my forehead and eyes so that I could dig the scene. Music was booming from outside speakers of record stores, as the rundown Datsun Taxi moved through the go-slow. The taxi could load and discharge passengers while on the way, because of the slow pace of traffic. We were now on a slight incline. I was lucky because I was in the front with the driver, so I did not have to be bothered by the loading and discharging of his passengers at the back. The light turned green and we were on the move through New Benin junction. The activities at the New Benin Market overflowed on the New Lagos Road, adding to the go-slow.

The traffic eased up as we moved past the police station, and in no time, the speed of the taxi increased. We passed the State School Board sign and in a matter of a few minutes, I was getting out of the taxi. My fare was 30 kobo, I paid it and entered the school grounds.

That day at school passed by quickly, as I made myself busy, looking through the school library for relevant books. I also got started on lesson plans for the new subject I was introducing into the school curriculum.

It did not take long before I found myself in the classroom. I had a heavy schedule, being the only teacher in my field, on the school staff.

Moving out of the hotel became a necessity as days, weeks and finally, some months passed by with us still in the hotel. There were many times when we would enter the dining room, only to meet the tables fully booked. There was a pattern to the activities in the hotel. The men, who were always older, who could be decribed as sugar daddies, brought in young and pretty women. The women would eat dinner, but the men would be involved in drinking beer or stout.

On one Friday evening, we entered the dining room, and went up to the counter to ask if it was possible to place a call to California. The receptionist said that the phone could only be used for local calls. I was about to explain to her about my need to place the call, when a tipsy brother started staggering towards the spot where my wife was standing. I dropped the conversation and rushed over to my wife, just in time to put myself in the path of the man who had had too much to drink. Once the fellow noticed the stern look on my face, he sobered up and staggered away. Meanwhile I heard someone asking the hotel clerk for a room. The women he was with, was smiling.

The next morning which was a Saturday, we dressed up and hit the streets. We had had our last straw with hotel life. We wanted to move into our own place. I remembered how good my wife could cook and so, we were going to locate a place, using our own initiative. The School Bursar had also been looking for a house for us. We chartered a taxi for two hours, for-N5.00.

I told the driver our mission, and we headed toward G.R.A. The G.R.A. stands for Government Reservation Area, which, in colonial times was an area of the town reserved for Europeans, also known then as European Quarters. The beautiful houses and flats in this part of Benin were nice. We had no idea of what the school would pay for our housing, so we decided to look at only what we thought was reasonable.

The first small bungalow, we looked at, was adequate, if not exciting. We met the landlord's representative who told us that we could move In as soon as the school paid them a year's rent of-N5000 in advance. Our time with the chartered taxi was almost up, so we started back to our hotel.

On Monday, I informed the Principal about the flats and houses we had sighted and the range of rent being asked. He was quite surprised and said that such a huge amount was out of the question.

He thought it was quite funny for us to have looked at houses that high. He said that one flat had been found and that we should go and look at the place. It was a building with four apartments in it. It was a two-bedroom apartment that had some things about it that we did not like. It had a nicely painted living and dining room, and it was very airy. The bedrooms were manageable. The bathroom proved to be the hitch. The door to the bathroom was only five feet high. That meant I would have to bend my six-foot frame drastically, to enter the bathroom. Once in, I found that there was no hot water heater nor bathtub, but a shower which we did not like.

The landlord was there to meet us and show us around, so we showed him what we did not like about the bathroom, and pointed out the basic corrections that I would need to make. He looked at us as though we were dreaming and refused to do anything to the place. That ended that.

The Principal was not happy to hear that we did not like the place. He said, "Your tastes are too high. Do you think you are in America?" He went on to tell me that the Indian expatriates in the school had been housed in similar flats, that cost 475.00 per month, and that rents had gone up in Benin. I informed him that I am not an Indian, and that the flat was just not my taste.

One day, one of my wife's new found friends, and a co-worker of hers, showed her a flat in the Ekewan area of Benin. It was a very nice cozy place, with only two apartments in the bungalow. It met all the basic requirements of a modern apartment. The price was slightly higher than the other place.

We went to see the Real Estate Agent who said that my school would never agree to pay that much, because the Principal would say that the house is too much for me. I told him that I was determined to take the flat as soon as possible. The agent was a stocky Nigerian. He sat back in his chair and said, "1 know that your Principal will never agree, but try anyway." He told me that he had studied in England and asked how I liked Nigeria. I told him that I could answer that question better after I had settled down. He responded by saying, "Why' don't I send you a nice Benin girl to be your second wife?" I asked him if he had two, and he informed me that he had only one wife. We both had a good laugh.

I could not wait for the next day to arrive, when I would inform the Principal about the house my wife and I had found. Living in a hotel indefinitely was a drag. I was really beginning to miss my wife's cooking and we received positive signs that at least some of the hotel staff had become cold, maybe tired of serving us everyday.

I arrived at school with my wife and a big smile. Getting there was a drag, because my long legs were squeezed in the back of the Datsun 120. We trekked the distance, after coming down from the taxi on the road, from New Lagos Road towards the new campus of the school. The old campus was on the opposite side of the road from the new campus, however it was waterlogged. We reached the reception area and waited for a chance to see the principal. There was a short wait, after which we were called into the principal's office. We exchanger greetings in the African way with respect. The Principal sat back in his seat as I presented a letter to him from the Realtor, stating the offer and details of the flat I wanted to occupy.

He looked up at me after reading the letter and said, "You refused the flat the school found for you." I responded quickly by saying that in fact it was the landlord who refused to make the place suitable. The Principal's response was on the tip of his tongue, and he said, "The school can not pay this great amount." My wife quickly responded by saying, "Does that mean that we should live in a place that is not up to our standard?" The Principal then said, "Why do you people prefer low density areas like Ekewan area?" Don't you know rents are higher there? I told him in a firm voice that we have located a standard accommodation and that there was no need for him to waste time. The loud discussion took a form of an argument, with the Principal remaining indifferent to the situation. I decided that it was a waste of time to discuss it with him any further. So I cut the argument off very abruptly, and grabbed my wife by the hand. We left.

I sat down that afternoon after waiting for two hours at the School Board. The high officials acted as though they were far too busy to worry about my problem. I composed a letter, stating my situation and how I wanted to leave the hotel. I also included my feeling that it would be a waste of government money for us to remain in the hotel, listing how much was being wasted on our accommodation in comparison to how little they could pay for a place for us.

Late the following morning, after getting the letter typed at the school, I presented the letter to the Principal and asked for his signature: He read the letter carefully and looked surprised by its contents. He said, "Well, I cannot sign this letter. It will implicate the school." I told him that I was ready to take the letter in its present form to the Military Governor of the State. He took a deep breath and looked at me as though I deserved the respect of a victorious opponent. He said, "Please delete the lines I have marked and when I see the adjusted letter, I will sign it and write out a check for your flat." So I had the letter adjusted, deleting the lines that he felt might implicate him and the school. The school clerk had it retyped and later that day, I gave it to the Principal. He signed it and gave me the check which I was to give to the Real Estate agent.

The man at the agency, whom I had talked to before, was surprised to see me with the check, and he was proud of my .efforts in squeezing the money out of the Principal. I began to think about a lot of things, like what I would have to do in the next couple of days. I knew I would be getting down in Benin City.

AIRPORT IN BENIN

At the African airport
In old sweet Benin
See the women
In their prettiest things

The wrappers and the dresses
The Mrs. And the Misses
In ole sweet Benin
See the passengers, relatives
And friends
But only the passengers are flying

50 kobo parking fee
or trek in on your feet
The jet will land and turn around
Before the flight out of town

Then there is a short bus ride
Load up and the take off stride
Just to leave sweet Benin
The women wear their pretty things

CHAPTER 16

Enjoying Nigeria

A DAY IN JUNE

Green is the grass, the day overcast
The rainy season is here at last
Gallops become mini ponds
Rain some more, let the food grow

Farmers are happy,
the weather is cool
Roasted corn on the cob,
the end of school

Sunshine sneaks in,
kissing the motorists and pedestrians
Ikebes are moving, tempting good men

The girls are back from far off schools
The town is 'live, watch their moves
Sunshine is broken by a tropical rain
While traders hustle for their tarpauline

The school was very good about providing the necessities for getting started. The school provided me with a refrigerator, and a gas stove or 'cooker' as the Nigerians call it. For the living room and dining room, four chairs, a couch, in addition to a dining table with six chairs were all provided. I added my furniture which arrived from America, and found my little duplex was slightly overcrowded, however, it was very cozy and comfortable.

The Ekewan area where we lived, had clean air, and the grass, a lush green, in this developing area that had been vacant bush, fifteen years ago. Although Ekewan road was the major road in the area, the dirt roads inside the Ekewan area, proved tough as the first rains appeared, making the roads very muddy. As I made my way towards the main road, one morning, I got soaked by the heavy downpour. Poto-poto or mud destroyed many of my shoes. The rain in this part of Africa is warm, unlike the cold rain in San Francisco.

The accommodation problem had taken too much of my time. I had a big job in getting acquainted with the new school I had become part of. I had to acquaint myself with a new syllabus, schedule, procedure, and the Nigerian secondary school system, and my students. Transportation to and from school was strictly by taxi. The school van should have been picking me up, but it was definitely in need of repairs.

During my first couple of classes, introducing my subject to the students, some of them complained about my intonation. They said, "Please sir, we do not understand slang." Their reference to 'slang' was how they interpreted the way Afroans speak American English. I would speak in a very loud and clear voice and I know most of them could understand what I was saying. Those students complaining about my 'slang' were only letting me know that they were aware of the fact that I was not a Nigerian.

My assignment in my school, was to introduce Government as a course of study in that school. Nigeria was only beginning to re-emerge after a 14-year period of military rule. A new civilian government, using the presidential system, was taking over. My intense interest in Africa and African Affairs made my task very easy. My experience of growing up in a black urban environment in San Francisco, made understanding the dynamics of urban distractions to the attention of students very easy.

My excellent understanding of broken English or Pidgin, began to pay off in Naira and Kobo. My intonation improved, because, for example, the going rate per drop by taxi was 10 kobo, however, if a taxi driver heard a foreign accent, even on the Pidgin English, his price would go up, to 50 kobo or one Naira. That also went for any item I wanted to purchase. If a trader knew that I was a foreigner, the price of the item I wanted to purchase, would be jacked up. So my knowledge of broken English came in very handy.

Another advantage in my understanding Pidgin, was that I could always hear what my students were saying under their breath in class. They would say things like, "1 no dey hear dis oyibo." Others would say that they do not understand this American or Jamaican.

I began to make many friends. Some were professionals and graduates. Some were my agemates, while others were much older. It was an agemate that showed me around. We would charter taxis, as though money did not mean a thing, through the streets of Benin. This also gave me a chance to see how people drive in Benin.

I was eligible for a car loan from the State Board of Education. As time passed by, I was forced to step up my efforts to get the car loan, which was my right. Taxi fares were rising, and it was getting too expensive to charter them at random.

One bureaucrat felt that I was pushing too hard for my car loan. He formed a personal hatred for me, but it did not bother me, because I knew that I had not done anything to him, to deserve the hatred. I pushed hard, because I found out that being an expatriate or being on contract was just not enough. One has to be aggressive in Nigeria if they want something done.

I secured the help of one of my friends to get my car loan. In the meantime, the car I had wanted to buy was sold, due to the unnecessary delay caused by that bureaucrat. I searched all over Benin for a car to buy, finding out that I would have to sign up on one-year waiting lists in most of the major dealerships. I needed a car right away because I had to escape walking on the muddy side roads caused by the heavy rains. In desparation, I unceremoniously bought a Volkswagen 1500. My brother-in-law who had just arrived from the U.S.A. went with me to buy it. He drove the car away from the car dealership because I did not know how to drive a stick shift; I was used to automatic transmission cars, which were not being sold in Benin. He drove toward our Ekewan area house, while I watched. About four blocks from the house, I stopped him and took the wheel. I stumbled along, having no previous experience driving a non-automatic transmission vehicle.

Being back on wheels, I knew, would give me the chance to enjoy Nigeria and Benin in particular. It took me no time at all to master how to drive the Volkswagen, changing gears and getting used to stepping on the clutch, while doing so. My mind went back to the time my family lived on South Ridge Road in the Hunters' Point Projects or La Salle Street, in San Francisco. I remembered the big trucks that used to move up La Salle Street, towards the hilltop and back down the same street towards the white areas, they had come from. The sound of the trucks changing gears was a childhood song for my brothers and I. All of us would emulate the sounds of the gears changing: u-u-uen strag (1st gear), u- u-uen strag (2nd gear), u-u-uen strag (3rd gear), and so on. Using that system, I pressed the clutch at exactly the right time and I became an expert on the little four-speed Volks.

Traffic jams or go-slows in Benin City, were found at various major junctions and during the time, I was still new at the wheel, I avoided the Akpakpava- New Lagos Road junction and the New Lagos-Mission Road junction. My little Volks absorbed the bumps and dives of some of the biggest gallops or pot-holes in the roads.

There are many cars on the streets of Benin, and I noticed them better when I started driving. There were many Mercedes Benz models, old and brand new, ranging from the sports models to the 280 and 450 series. The big models were supposed to be banned, but I saw many of them. In Nigeria, the Mercedes Benz is the equivalent of a Cadillac to Afroans, The Peugeot 504 seems to be the well to-do man's car. There were Toyotas, old Opels, Fiats, Ladas and Datsuns, to name a few of the cars. There were a few Volvos which were supposed to be some type of status symbol in Nigeria. The Russian 'mercedes' as the Volga is called, commands respect because of its big size on the roads where small cars are the majority.

Driving my Volks through Benin gave me a chance to really see Benin. While on the road, one has to be ready for anything, because careless driving could put one into big trouble. Still, there are many people who feel that they own the roads, expecting everyone else to stop for them. Horns were blaring at full blast, blending in with the heat of the blazing sun, while a white 504.

CHAPTER 17

The Road to Nkwerre

THE IRONY OF IT ALL

The Irony of it all
You rise and you fall
The Blacks were standing tall
UNTIL Our downfall

The scars are deep
What's your's you keep
It's white domination
Or Black Liberation

It is general knowledge that before one attempts to make an interstate trip, the car must be in good shape. I started out too late to get the Volga properly serviced. At that point, I took my car in to the main dealership, but they would not take on any more business that day. It was at this time that I acquainted myself with a very nice Ishan mechanic, who put my car in good shape. I was advised that my tires needed to have weights put on them, which would cost about -N-15.00, but I did not heed to the advice. Otherwise, my car was in perfect shape for the trip.

We headed for Nkwerre with the music in the car, sounding good. My wife was very happy to go to her hometown, but I wondered what the villagers would have to say. As much as we tried to have an early start, we started our trip around 12:30 p.m. My tank was full. I turned from College Road on to Ekewan Road, continuing until I entered Ring Road, Benin's big circular street that has streets leading from the ring to all major streets of Benin City. We rounded the ring, spinning out on Akpakpava Street. We continued down Akpakpava Street towards the New Lagos Road junction. The big traffic jam which is the order of the day, slowed us down. As soon as the traffic light flashed green, all of the cars were off, going down Ikpoba Slope. As we approached Ikpoba River I looked at the old bridge that looked ancient in contrast to the new bridge which we were driving on. We continued after crossing the bridge up Ikpoba Hill, until it changed into the highway to Asaba.

The road turned out to be a complete descent, as if Benin City sat up at the top of a high plateau. We continued cruising at 80 km. to 100 km. per hour. The car ran smoothly, while the music in the car was groovy. We had only traveled 5 to 10 miles, when I noticed that all of the cars in front of me were coasting, slowing down, and finally stopping. By now, a long line of cars had been formed. It was like being in the middle of a Benin go-slow. It was not a go-slow being five to ten miles out of Benin City, instead I found out that it was a Police road-block. The Police were checking the particulars - registration, insurance and licenses of the cars. I noticed that some of the cars behind me quickly turned around and started back towards Benin. We waited until it was our turn and two young policemen asked me for the particulars. I showed them, and we were waved on.

We were back on the road to Imo State. I remember Umunede, the village with all the yams for sale. It is an Ibo-speaklng area. The bush and fertile green land around showed that it is a land, rich in what is needed to grow food. We stopped and my wife spoke her language to one of the traders, and this made the price of the yams much cheaper. I had to stay back in the car, so that I would not ruin her chances of getting the yams at the cheapest price. If I had gone up there, I could see the traders saying, "Money dey for him body Oh..." meaning that I look to them like someone with a lot of money; that jacks up the price. So I made sure that I made myself invisible, counting all the taxis as they zoomed pass, racing with each other, and at times, risking the lives of their passengers.

My wife was back With a lot of yams. She got a deal that would have been impossible to get in Benin City. We loaded the yams in the large trunk of Benin City's only red Volga. We took off, continuing our journey, with the cassette playing one of my favorite Reggae songs. The long two-lane highway was very smooth. Our only problem came from the slow-moving lorries, laden with goods or cement. When it was time to overtake the stow vehicles, I realized the possible hazard of two-lane highways. Passing is always dangerous.

The record, 'Madness' by the Reggae group, The Maytones, had just finished Playing on the cassette, when my wife told me that we would soon reach Asaba, a town located on the western bank of the Niger River. She was right, as the kilometer markings on concrete road signs showed that there were only a few kilometers left before we would get to Asaba. I asked her how she knew and she told me that she used to pass that same road from the East to Lagos, way back, during her high school days.

It was only minutes before we entered the road leading to the modern bridge over River Niger. Naturally, we took some pictures of the river, as we crossed the bridge. It is an understatement to say that it is only a beautiful river. It is magnificent. Once across the bridge we were in Anambra State and the first town we got to right off the bridge was Onitsha, located on the eastern bank of the River Niger. River Niger is the natural boundary between Bendel State and Anambra State.

We were now in the old Eastern Region, headed for my wife's village. The land seemed a little different from Bendel State. The vegetation was not as thick and it was a bit drier, judging from the brownish-green foliage. The soil was brown in contrast to the red soil in Benin City. We were now on the road to Owerri, which is the capital of Imo State and a few miles to Nkwerre. The good road made the trip quick, and soon we were entering Owerri. Suddenly, the tarred road turned into a dusty dirt road, that was smooth enough to be tarred.

My wife used her language to ask directions to Nkwerre, because she had been away for a long time, and there were three different ways to get there. We went the shortest cut, and after circling around, we were back on the highway again. One thing about Imo State is that it Is heavily populated. People were all over the place. There were all kinds of festivities going on in the villages we were passing through. The masqueraders called 'Ekpo' were out performing. It is a way of tying In the culture on the one day of the year that most people are back In their hometowns or villages, from the various cities all over the country. The signboards we saw along the way, indicated the names of the big towns and villages, giving my wife sweet and bitter memories of how she used to travel through them in her past.

As we approached Nkwerre, we found ourselves in a rush to beat nightfall, while I focused my attention on the jagged road. My mind took short breaks from the tedious driving, to reflect on the fact that my wife, like every Nigerian, has a village - a place where people speak her dialect of her language. I know that I will never forget the road to Nkwerre.

CHAPTER 18

The Native Law and Custom Marriage

CELEBRATING OUR CULTURE

Celebrate our being
Celebrate our culture
Celebrate our soul
Celebrate our role

Celebrate our land
Where we come from
Celebrate our Africa
Africans in America

Understand what existed
Before the white man
Understand our history
In our Black ancestral land

We were only a few miles from Nkwerre, when we spotted some young guys washing cars near a stream. Our car was dusty, so we pulled over and my wife negotiated with the guys to have our car washed. The cost was to be ~1-1.50. We stood aside while the exterior of our car received a good wash. After the guys were finished, we paid them and they were very glad. Just as we were entering the car to continue our journey, we were greeted by an indigene of Nkwerre who sped off on a motorcycle.

Back on the road again, we were sure and confident of reaching Nkwerre before nightfall, because it was less than two miles away. My wife began pointing out the various landmarks she remembered.

We entered the town at dusk and instead of heat, we were met with a nice cool breeze. To my surprise, Nkwerre was not just a big collection of villages, but a developing township. Like most developing towns, there was a tarred main road running through the heart of the town.

We turned off at a dirt road that led us to a small family-run guest house. We parked in the driveway while my wife went to talk to the madam who runs the hotel. There was a warm embrace between my wife and her towns' lady, and then, an introduction so that the woman would know who I was. The hotel workers were instructed by her to carry our bags into our room, while we sat down and had our dinner. We checked into the hotel so that we would not be Imposing on anyone, even though my wife had her father's and mother's relatives resident in the town. The family house was there, but I felt that it would be better to stay in a neutral place.

The following morning, I loaded the drinks I had brought from Benin into the car and we drove to the family house, which was further down the tarred road. I drove Into the big compound and parked. We entered the two storied house and met the patriarch of the family. He was surprised to see us, because he did not know that we were coming. Although he was happy to meet me, he told me that custom is custom, meaning that I should be officially introduced to the senior members of my wife's family. He offered us drinks. The patriarch who also happens to be my wife's most senior uncle on her father's side, sent a message to the village square to summon the elders of my wife's family. In the meantime my father-in-law arrived from Zaria. He too was surprised to see us in Nkwerre. After the summons with a special native drum called Ekwe, about twelve senior gentlemen had arrived. I was introduced by my uncle-in-law to the elders. I then presented the drinks I had brought from Benin as gifts. There was a lot of talk going on in the Ibo language, and yet it was only an undertone. My father-in-law explained what I was saying to the elders, because some of them did not understand my intonation. Finally, the patriarch yielded to the floor to listen to what the elders had to say.

Most of the elders were 65 years old and older. They were dressed in various types of Ibo traditional outfits. Some were younger men on vacation from their jobs or businesses in the big cities. One of the elder men spoke first in Ibo and he seemed to reflect the general sentiment of the group when he finally said to me in English, "Young man, we are happy to meet you. When we heard that our daughter had married an American, we thought you would be white, but we are very happy to see that you are as black as we are. However, your marriage is an overseas marriage, therefore we do not recognize it." Another of the elders rose and spoke in a heavy Ibo accent, "Overseas marriages are null and void, unless you perform the Native law and Custom Marriage of our people." One by one, the elders began to speak, all with one theme t the customary marriage had to be performed.

After many drinks and informal conversation, my wife and I started to leave. On the way out, many of the elders asked us what plans we had for accommodation. We informed them that we were putting up in a hotel. Many of them said that they were insulted about the fact that their daughter was in a hotel in her own hometown, however, we politely refused the offers of accommodation. The final word of the highly educated patriarch, my wife's uncle was that our marriage would not be complete until the customary wedding was performed.

My wife and I drove back to our hotel and had a drink, after which we drove to her mother's family house and met many of my wife's maternal relatives. They were all very happy to meet me and served us a lot of drinks.

Early the next morning, we were prepared to return to Benin. We drove to my wife's father's compound to inform my father-in-law of our intention to return to Benin that day. After failing to convince us to stay one more day, he wished us a safe journey. It was early afternoon when we started back to Benin. We entered Owerri, enroute to Benin, via Onitsha. The Owerri- Onitsha Road provided a good drive, because the traffic was light and flowed at a good speed.

Finally, we approached the bridge which crosses the River Niger. There was a traffic jam caused by the Nigerian Police Force who had mounted up a check point at the Onitsha side of the bridge. One by one, cars were given permission to proceed, and those who did not have proper registration had to pull over, causing more traffic jam. A senior Police Officer waved us on and we were headed for the Asaba side of the bridge, and then the road to Benin.

It was 7:00 p.m. when we arrived at our Benin flat. The car had made it, but not without a struggle. We entered the house and went to bed.

The next year passed by quickly, teaching everyday in the high school. I kept having flashbacks of my trip to Nkwerre. I felt happy that they recognized my blackness in Nkwerre. I felt that it was an honor for me to be required to marry my wife, a daughter of Nkwerre, in a traditional ceremony.

During the first week of November, we received a letter from my wife's father, detailing instructions for the Customary Marriage. Although Imo State is an area known for high bride prices or dowry, the elders decided to spare me from a high bride price. That did not mean I was getting off free. A list of gifts for the men and women of my wife's family, was also provided by my father-in-law. My father-in-law stood to gain nothing materially, but wanted our marriage sanctioned. He acted as a moderating influence on those who wanted to make it expensive.

The list of items I was to take to Nkwerre to present to the people for the ceremony, was full of cultural significance. Meeting the conditions meant that my marriage would be recognized as legal in my wife's village. Ignoring the customary marriage would have made my wife's parents social outcasts in their village.

The conditions for the Customary Marriage were adjusted to fit my circumstances, because, in Nigeria, one brings his family to marry someone traditionally. Since I did not have any family members in the country, I took a delegation of friends. Among my friends was one other brother from the United States who also lived in BenIn. I asked him to follow me and he agreed without hesitation. Had it been that I was a Nigerian, I would have been turned back, because the elders would ask: "Where is your father and the elders in your family? Go and bring them, so that we can talk to them as agemates. You are too young to talk to us."

The date was set for January 4th, when my father-in-law would be in Nkwerre. My wife and her friend checked out all of the traditional markets to buy the required items, although I sponsored it financially. The truth of the matter was that if I was to go and buy the items, myself, the price would go up by 200%.

It was now December, which meant that it was examination period in the school. I had many sleepless nights, correcting students' essays, because my deadline was December 10th. The examination period was always very demanding. There would be many hours of watching over crafty students during invigilation. Some would go to any limits, trying to pass their exams.

I finished recording my grades and started preparing for my second journey to Nkwerre. I made several trips to my mechanic, putting my car in shape for the trip.

January 4th arrived just as I completed preparations and our two-car delegation began the trip to Nkwerre. In a developing country, things are always changing and the route to Nkwerre was no exception. The change was a good one. Instead of going through Owerri and entering Nkwerre from the south, we took a new road that entered Nkwerre from the north, cutting off the road with jagged edges.

Our journey in the Russian car would have been very regular, except that my cassette recorder, which had been fixed some days earlier, packed up. There was no music and the goat we were carrying along with us as one of the gifts, took up all the slack with its crying. The other brother from the States sat in the front of the car with me, while my wife and her friend sat in the back, with the goat on the floor. A lively conversation saved the ride from being a boring one. The rest of the delegation, an Nkwerre man, resident in Benin and his wife, followed us in their car.

We arrived in Nkwerre by way of Orlu, on a smooth road; a proof of the progress of a developing country. Our first stop was at the hotel where we had stayed the last time we were in Nkwerre. This time, the hotel was quiet because all of the excitement that marks the New Year had died down. My friend and I took our rooms and changed from our traveling clothes, while my wife and her friends went ahead to her village to make advance arrangements. My friend and I dressed in a hurry, while we waited for my wife who went to notify the patriarch of the family of our arrival.

Times have changed; a lot of things in a lot of places. West Africa and Nkwerre, in particular is no exception. In traditional times, visitors or natives of the land, who had been away for a very long time, were met on the outskirts of town and led into town with dancers, drumming and other welcoming activities. Nkwerre of today, with the county seat of Nkwerre-Isu Local Government Council, had changed. My arrival to Nkwerre was quiet and unnoticed.

My wife arrived back to the hotel just as I was coming out of my day-dreaming about history. I had finished dressing and after my wife hurriedly changed into a traditional outfit, she insisted that we should hurry up because everyone was waiting on me. She had already seen her father, but she was upset because her mother, my beloved mother-in-law, was unable to come from Zaria.

Our delegation arrived at my wife's family compound, in my overlaoded car which still stood out, since I did not see any other Volgas. We entered the first floor living room, the same living room where I had been introduced to the elders during my previous visit. There were about twenty elderly gentlemen, including my father-in-law who had come from over 500 miles away to be there. We were ushered towards an area of the living room. My friend created a lot of excitement and conversation because of his height. Our hosts brought out drinks to entertain us with and the atmosphere was ripe for Black Unity.

I remembered how I had been told a story in Benin, about how one man went to his girlfriend's family house to marry her and was overtaken by the hospitality of his hosts. While he was in the middle of a great meal, another suitor suddenly appeared and demanded the girl's hand in marriage. As if the elders could read my thoughts, a call to order was made. I surveyed the living room, looking at the full faces of the elders. More people were still arriving, and although there were now about thirty people present, there was room for more.

The patriarch began by informing everyone what the occasion was all about, and why it was necessary for the Customary Marriage to take place. I stood up to respond, saying that I felt it was an honor to marry their daughter in the traditional way. I also informed them that I had brought certain gifts which I wanted to present to them. Even though most of the elders understood English, my uncle-in-law made it a point of duty to translate what I had said into Ibo.

At this point, my friend, the other Nkwerre man who had accompanied us from Benin, and my wife's young nephews and cousins, helped to unload the car and bring in the cartons of liquor, snuff, cigarettes and the rest of the required items. The goat was tied to a tree outside the living room. Just as we assembled everything on the center table and on the floor, one of the elders stood up. He was overtaken by emotion and said, "So you were able to do all this? You are a man!" He went on to say that he was happy that I want to respect African customs.

My wife's senior uncle, the patriarch of the family, began to speak on the benefit of having solid family ties, connecting partners in a marriage. He explained the values that his village and tribe place on marriage. The atmosphere was very warm. My wife beamed with a bright smile as he continued. He concluded by saying that if ever, there were any marital problems between my wife and I, I should feel free to go to them to work out a solution.

The older men now started giving me words of advice in Ibo. My wife interpreted what was being said to me, however, I could also draw some conclusions by their gestures. The most common line was that marriage is looked upon as permanent. Many were surprised that I was able to value African institutions.

Another stage of the wedding was reached when drinks from among those I brought were opened. Some was poured on the ground by my wife's senior uncle, as libation, to symbolize giving our African ancestors their share of what was to be consumed. He gave a glass to my wife and said she should drink some of it and pass the rest to me, kneeling down in front of me to present it. By doing that, she was showing them who her husband is, because up till that time, I could not be recognized in that capacity, until the ceremony had been performed. The rest of the drinks I had brought were shifted to the other side of the spacious living room. The elders prayed for the success of our marriage, after which the patriarch rose to his feet and called on my wife to stand up. There was silence in the living room, while he sat her down on my lap. Everyone burst into laughter of joy. This was the final act of this phase of tying the knot, African Style. Food, drinks and merriment followed.

One of the older women reminded me that I had now taken care of the requirements for the men, but that I should not forget the women, I responded philosophically by saying, "In Africa, we never finish marrying." I agreed.

African Moon

AFRICAN MOON

I have sat under the African sun
My body soaking wet from its heat
We Blacks sit under the African sun
With black tempered skins, no sunburn

I have sat under the African moon
Counting the stars
Thinking of my people's forced journey afar
Where some don't know who they are

I have sat under the African moon
On African dirt, my land
From one end of the night
Until the coming of a morning sunlight

I have sat thinking
I have sat feeling
The power of being Black
Wondering where is our power to act

I have sat under Africa's moon
Hoping liberation would come soon
Hoping for the liberation of my people
Sitting under my African moon

Closing thoughts and true stories and poems

Journey to the Motherland

A journey by air
A journey to share

Journey if you dare
Follow me and go there
Journey to our motherland
By a San Francisco born Black Man

This part is a true story
To see what my land would show me
About a San Francisco homie
Some of you know me

My journey to Nigeria
By way of Liberia
North, South, East and West
I Liked the Midwest best

My journey started in Lagos
Traveled North to Kaduna/Zaria/Kano
Traveled south to Benin and Port H
Then the East always promoting peace

Journey to my land
Journey to feel and understand
Journey to our ancestor's land
Journey to our motherland.

As the 1980 primaries for the democrats unfolded, I found myself a regular quest analyst on the weekly news program called The International News Review a television program. These appearences made me very popular in Benin..

When the primaries ended and Vernon Jordon, former head of the Urban League was shot in the back, I was called to the International News Review to discuss the African-American reaction to that shooting of a Black leader by a white racist while that leader was in the company of a white woman in the wee hours of the night.

What must be said about Nigerian-African-American relationships is that Nigerians in Nigeria on the average displayed a far greater interest in what goes on in the world affecting African People including African-Americans.

Popularity has it's ups and downs in Nigeria. Many times as I approached police check points which replaced military check points as Nigeria prepared for the 1979 presidential constitution and civilian government some police would wave me through because they would say they had seen me on TV.

Many White Americans expressed fear of what I said on Nigerian television about the abuses of African-Americans by police and America's colonial relationship with my African-American brothers and sisters. These fears were expressed to my late wife and were based on fears of how Nigerians would respond to my comments.

As 1981 approached I began discussing the idea of returning to America with my wife. It was in some ways a tug of war within me.. As an African- American freedom fighter, free in Nigeria, I yearned to rejoin my family and our struggle for dignity and liberation in America. There was also a tug of war within my wife because she also wanted to pursue a PHD in the USA.

The Bendel State School Board Secretary, similar to the California State Superintendent of Pulic Schools in California summoned me upon receiving notification that I had planned to return to the USA. When I arrived at his office he greeted me and we sat down. He asked me if I was sure about wanting to go back to the USA? I explained my decision. The Secretary then said "If I wanted to sign another contract I could be named a vice principal in a rural high school and receive a big pay raise.

I felt really good about this offer which I felt resulted from my being a good government teacher. Even though contributing to the development of African youth in Nigeria was a contribution to African People all over the world, I began to yearn to make my contribution to African-Americans, some who doubted their real identity in my African-American communities in America.

I also longed for my family, my brothers and sisters. My mom. My dads and fathers. I missed them all.

I thanked the secretary for his generous offer and began preparing to return to America where I probably would not be invited to the TV station. In August of 1981 I returned to America. My wife and I.

When I returned to the USA, we moved to San Jose 50 miles south of San Francisco to be close to my family and the support needed to readjust. I really tried to make my way in the south bay but unless you had computer skills they were not yet ready to practice equal opportunity. Never the less I completed the first edition of this book in San Jose and met up with an old movement buddy who had a print shop. Well I sent the manuscript to many publishers and received many rejection letters. Finally I invested my resources and self published the first edition. That was quite an experience. First I was too informal with the printer making the deal over dinner and a handshake. The original price was $3200. For 2000 copies. However because I had no contract the so called friend raised the price to $5200 and since I had no contract or even a written estimate I learned a very good lesson.

I did some some things right on that first edition and enjoyed some successes. My title The Black Expatriate in Africa proved hard to understand in the USA because the word is not widely used here.

As a good salesman I distributed the book very well and appeared on many Bay Area television and radio programs.

I went for it by taking a bus to New York City in July 1982 staying with some Black liberation freedom fighters there close to the East Cultural Organization.

I was interviewed on a radio station and I had a table at the African Street Fair held at the Boys and Girls High School Yard. There I sold more than 250 books. From there I took a bus to Washington DC and had a book party at Brother Ali's Pyrimid Bookstore right out side of Howard University. I also had a radio interview on a public radio station in Washington D.C. and sold many books. I also distributed books to the Black Modana Bookstores centered in Detroit and Hakim's Books which were located in Philadelphia and Atlanta. Midwest Area Sales and Services sold many copies tin the Chicago area.

Additional copies were sold to the Bookstores of the University of the West Indies in Trinidad and Jamaica. Locally I had many book signing sessions at B. Daltons Bookstores. However Marcus Books sold many copies.

The highest honor given to this book was when the Schomberg Collection of Rare Black Books which is associated with the New York Public Library System requested a copy. As it turned out the first edition really became rare. I only have the original manuscript and I copy of the book. My older brother Darnell had kept a copy and before he gave me that copy of the original edition in 1999 it was only a dream remembered.

!983-1990

In 1983 I began a new career in community services at the Oceanview Merced Ingleside Community Association which provided the foundation for the OMI-Pilgrim Community Center.

Although I started out with a very low salary supervising the Summer Youth Employment and Training Program my biggest challenge was taking care of my wife whose blood pressure problems became more servere. In early 1984 Chinwe's kidneys shut down. Luckily for me community services flexibility allowed me to take her to dialysis Mondays, Wednesdays and Fridays on my late lunch break and pick her up after work.

The late Mr. I.T.Bookman and other board members hired me to supervise the OMI Summer Youth Employment and Training where I prepared hundreds of OMI youth for the labor market with their first summer job. After a period of observation Mr. Bookman introduced me to the OMI- Pilgrim Community Center Board and I became board secretary.

Chinwe's health was my number 1 priority and she hung in there throughout 1984 . Chinwe was very excited when her mother visited us in May 1985. However Chinwe suffered a stroke on May 13,1985 and passed away May 31,1985. I was devastated and my friend Mr. Bookman died 2or 3 days later. Chinwe passed away at 33 and Mr. Bookman passed at 77.

I continued to try to keep going by focusing on building and completing the community center. I was elected Board president in 1986 and became great grantwriter writing all grant requests raising nearly 2 million dollars to build and operate the community center for the next 10 years. In late 1985 I also began writing a column BLACK POLITICS IN THE EIGHTIES for the Sun Reporter newspapers until 1990 In May of 1986 while 7 African-American carpenters were framing the community center 2 white police shot Larry Lumpkin a young Black man to death in highly questionable circumstances. A justice concerned citizens committee was formed to seek justice. That committee evolved into the SF Black United Front.

All of these factors gave me new areas to focus on but my heart was still in pain missing Chinwe. In 1990 I remarried to Sharon Clark but it did not last long,3 or 4 months…

The experience gained from working with the family of Larry Lumpkin and the brothers and sisters who were members and supporters of the San Francisco Black United Front was a great experience. We sought justice for the family and supported other African-American causes in San Francisco. I will always remember the Black Student Unions, the Pan African Student Union and the San Francisco Black United Front.

In 1989 I was named the Executive Director of the community center. OMI was always known as Lakeview is one of 4 neighborhoods I grew up in .I also spent my childhood in Fillmore, Crocker Amazon Projects, Hunters Point Projects before finally moving with my family to Lakeview.

I feel my work of developing the potential of African- American youth was and still is very important with all the threats to our existence posed by our situation.

African people all over the world have one destiny and similar problems . We face the question of liberation and development in differing dimensions.

As long as African People are oppressed by the west and our own inability to unite we must continue to struggle to improve ourselves to claim our destiny as a free and developed people. An as long as people are oppressed any where there will be a threat to people everywhere including Africa and African People.

JOURNEY TO THE MOTHERLAND

Journal to the motherland

A journey by air
A journey to share
Journey if you dare
Follow me and go there
Journey to the motherland
By a San Francisco
born Black Man

Mythical Africa

When` I wrote the first edition, I was much more interested in telling the story of my friendships and relationships with a proud modern Africa. Is there a mythical past and present? I wanted to tell the story about traffic jams and other aspects of Nigeria's modern side. I had my encounters and contacts which would be better as a magical or mythical Africa. Africa is as deep as the deepest river.

Upon further reflection I can see in the year 2000, that this omission while done for admirable reasons considering how Africa, our homeland has been treated by some sectors of the USA's media such as the Tarzan view of Africa proponents. However this omission of my encounters while done for admirable reasons omits an essential part of the journey. Every culture has it's own myths and mythologies.

I remember walking around in Benin City before I was able to complete my car loan application. While I was living at the Edo Guest House on Akpakpava Road and New Lagos Road. I remember being given that chalet until the school I was assigned to could find or approve a house for my late wife and I.

I walked down the street to a junction where there was an African Tree Company. I met a young Nigerian as I walked and he began to listen to me talk about some of the things I did not like about how my people were treated by the American government and society. (Has it really Changed when they get away with the murder of Amadou Diallo in New York City?)

This Nigerian young man began describing the power of the Blackman that was more powerful than the power of the Whiteman. He said if I was ready to join his secret society, I would see some of of the wonders of Black Power. At this point I asked him to give me an example of what he was talking about.

He said imagine seeing 20 people riding up to 400 feet in the air on a ... I never saw that man again in the years I lived in Benin City.

To Kill A Snake or Not

I remember where I lived in the Ekenwan area of Benin City. My house was located about 10 blocks to the edge of town. The land and the forest lay beyond those 10 blocks which had a tarred road. Even in Africa animals do not like to be around people or their cities. People are dangerous neighbors to animals.

However, I was driving to my house with my late wife. We were about 3 or 4 blocks from our house when we stopped in time to see a large snake crossing the road in front of my voltswagen1500 model. As the snake crossed I thought of running over the snake. My late wife said I do not believe all of the stories I hear about people transforming themselves into various types of animals. But this is Africa! The snake crossed the road and we drove home.

One day I was at home alone when I heard my African neighbor Omo, a brother from the Etsako tribe of northern Bendel State. His voice grew louder and louder. There was a snake in our compound . Omo's 4 bedroom bungalow and my 4 bedroom house were on 1 gated compound separated by 25 to 30 feet. I came out of my house. I saw my neighbor and another Nigerian standing next to a loose cement block, ironically the only loose block on our compound. I had an idea that took me all the way back to Hunters Point on Southridge Road where I grew up. I saw a milo can (a chocalate drink mix) can and a long plank. I remembered launching a rock that hit me in the eye as a kid in Hunters Point. But this was serious. I was told that the snake was poisonous green mambo about 4 to 5 feet ;long. I grabbed the 2' by 8' plank and balanced the wood on the can.

I was real careful. I picked a 5 feet length of pipe and placed the wood on the loose cement block. I caused the snake to come out when I stood on the wood and shook the cement block for the third time.

The snake began to raise his head with it's poisonous tongue extended. I used the steel pipe to crash and bash the snake. I knocked the snake in the head at least 50 times. I knew this snake was dead however this battle was not over. At this point a crowd of Nigerians arrived and cut the snake into two pieces. The head section was buried on 1 side of the road and the tail section was buried on the other side of the road. These sections of the snake were cut up 50 times. When I asked why, I was told the snake was cut up and buried on separate sides of the road so the snake could not join itself back together. Africa is Black..

I tell these stories of my personal experiences with a mythical aspect of Nigeria, a great African country. Nigeria is the ancestral home probably for the great majority since no other area was called slave like Nigeria was by the British colonialists.

The Nigeria I lived in was modern and the population was highly educated, rooted in their/our culture and home language, fluent in English and sometimes German, French many local languages and even distant African languages. Modern and Traditional Africa live side by side in Nigeria.

MY BOUT WITH MALERIA AND STORIES ABOUT ENCOUNTERS WITH NIGERIAN POLICE

I had my first encounter with Malaria before I left for Nigeria in a Nigerian party where I ran into a Nigerian who was an American trained medical doctor.

This Nigerian doctor like most other Nigerians in our circle had heard that Chinwe and I were going to Nigeria. The Nigerian doctor asked me if I was going to take anti-malaria pills before traveling to Nigeria? I turned the question around and asked him if I should?

He said, "that if I was going for 6 weeks or even 6 months take the pills before you leave and after you come back and there would be no problem.

He said further " that if I was going to stay for a year or more I should consider the option of allowing the malaria to get in your body so you could build up resistance to malaria. He warned that staying a long time might cause a big deadly attack.

I considered the advice seriously and took all of the required or recommended shots at UC Medical Center in San Francisco. a place I worked while I attended U.S.F.. I did not take any anti-malaria pills. I read about Mongo Park, a British explorer who died from malaria along with the rest of his crew of exploiters while sailing down the Niger River. Many Nigerians credit the mosquitoes in Nigeria (whose bite causes malaria) with saving Nigeria from the type of settler colonialism of the type that occupied Southern Africa.

I fell sick with what turned out to be malaria when I had been in the country of Nigeria for about 13 days. I was in Zaria walking around with Chicozia, my late wife's youngest brother. I fell while walking across a dry ditch.

When I returned to my in-law' s house, I began to throw up. I threw up food, water, soda or any thing else my in-law's brought to me. I even threw up water.

At that moment I thought about my wife who was in Lagos with her mother trying to take possession of our furniture we had shipped from the USA to Nigeria.

My late wife's father,two baby sisters and brother brought food even salad but I threw it up I continued to throw up water.

Finally my father in -law, a biology lecturer (in the school which had provided him with a4 bedroom modern campus house) decided that he needed to take me to the hospital. I was out of it. You know feeling really weak. They took me to ABU or Ahmada Bello University Hospital in Zaria. There a doctor examined me, diagnosed me, and gave me a shot with a real long needle. It was an anti-malaria shot.

I went back to their house that evening and continued to throw up everything for a week and a half. I had another anti-malaria shot and lost a lot of weight.

I also had fever including hot flashes where I sweated and sweated and chills where every thing was ice cold. I had no sexual energy which was very unusual for me. Only GOD saved me.

My late wife returned the day I started to fell better and she had great news. Our furniture had arrived and was stored in her cousin's garage.

We relocated to Benin City with in a month . I began to gain some of my weight back but not all of it. I had lost over 40 pounds but thanks to my in- law's I survived.

In Nigeria malaria is looked at like flu and some call it fever. Most Nigerians take anti-malaria medicine every Sunday medicine. After that first attack I began taking Sunday medicine every Sunday. For a long time I did not have any problem.

I was in Benin about 6or 7 months before I had another malaria attack but this time it was different.

I fell sick after teaching one Friday afternoon. My wife did not take me to a hospital. And although I felt weak, I was not throwing up very often nor did I feel as sick as I did up North in Zaria.

A good friend of my late wife who lived in the Ekenwa area with her husband came by with two big bags of leaves and a pot.

She explained that the leaves were the Dogonyaro tree leaves in 1 bag and 1 bag full of orange and lemon tree leaves. She explained to me that these Dogonyaro leaves were used by Nigerians to fight off malaria attacks and the orange and lemon tree leaves were meant to sweeten the medicine so an American tongue could swallow it.

This big pot of leaves boiled for 1 or 2 hours. I went back to bed while my wife and her friend stayed in the kitchen of our place. I had no energy once again.

Finally my wife came to our bedroom and led me to the kitchen. By now all of the leaves had boiled down.

First they poured a cup of the liquid from the pot into a big mug and covered it up. Next I was given a big towel and told to cover my head over the pot and inhale the vapors. I inhaled the steam for 20 to 30 minutes.

I started sweating but only a little at fist. Next I was told to take the cooled water. Liquid from the pot and take a bath with it. I took a bath. Lastly I drank the liquid in the covered mug. After drinking the herb tea I went slept like a baby.

I woke up early that next morning feeling great. I could see that malaria had drained out of my body leaving an outline of my body wet with sweat on the sheets.

Throughout the rest of my stay in Nigeria, I only had a few more attacks And each time I got malaria those Leaves worked thank GOD.

In 1984 when I caught the flu, I thought I was having a relapse of malaria. I ran to UC Medical Center's Tropical Clinic. The examined me and did some blood work but assured me that since I left Nigeria 3 years ago if I had a relapse he would write about it in the medical journals. The flu left in a few days.

Experiences with Nigerian police

My first experience with Nigerian police occurred after I hand only been in the Nigeria a few days. We were living in A Lagos superb called Ikeja. I took one of my solo walks. I felt almost at home immediately was walking down Isheri Road now called Chief Awolowo Road now.

I was walking in a big crowd of people when I accidentally stepped on the heel of a Nigerian policeman. Before my good manners could kick in I had traveled back to the USA in thought. I thought about how much trouble I could have been faced with if I stepped on the heel of an American policeman. You know what I mean.

Finally the policeman brought me back to Africa by saying sir I'm sorry, I'm sorry. I could not believe my ears or my eyes. I owed the apology. I had my culture shock. I was in the home of the Black Race. All of the historical fear and other fellow Africans experience in the USA had played itself out. And yet in a free Black Country that load was lifted.

Taken to court

In late 1979 after my first vacation going back to the USA, I had another episode with the Nigerian police. There are occaisonal roadblocks mounted by the police and sometimes, as is a sort of culture I sometimes keep cigarets in my car to give to police at roadblocks. Sometimes if you give 1or 2 sticks they would wave you through. Other times when I appeared on Nigerian Television in Benin either reading a poem or commenting on some important Pan African issue or news item. In the days that would follow that appearance I would pull up to a police roadblock people would wave me through while checking the registration of others. They would say in Nigerian broken English " No be you where we see for TV, Oga sir, You can pass.

However one day there was a shuffle by the Nigerian Police Force, a federal police force. These out or town police guys mounted checkpoints all over town. I was stopped 1 or 2 times and realized this was a special operation.

I was on my way to school when I was taken into custody and taken directly to the court. My wife was also taken to the same court. The problem was we did not have registration and Nigerian Drivers Licenses.

The police could have taken us to jail or arrested us. I asked the magistrate I appeared before if I could make a phone call to my principal and he said yes. By the way my school had a new principal Mr. A. Ayarre, a Benin Native who was also a socialist opposition leader. Mr. Ayarre received my call with a laugh

He said he would make some phone calls in our behalf and get our case shifted to a magistrate he knew who would handle this matter for you. My wife was a government official at the Ministry of Education but my principal's phone calls saved the day.

By noon we were called before another magistrate the magistrate told us to obey the laugh and proceeded to give us a mini lecture. Next the magistrate excused my wife and told her to go to the local DMV and return in 2 to 3 hours with a drivers license and car registration

I was released an hour later with same instructions.

By the time I arrived at the motor vehicles department and secured my registration my next task was to get in the diver's license line and fill out the application. When it was my turn the Nigerian official looked at me and looked at my application again and said in broken English No be your wife where task this test today I said yes OH. The brother then said" Okay-o- I go sign your paper. If your wife fit drive, you self go sabi drive. In other words if your wife can pass the driving test and she passed the driving test less than an hour ago then you can pass the test and there is no need wasting time. I went back to court with my documents and the magistrate dismissed my case too.

I gave my principal a bottle of Brandy as a way of saying thanks.

The Last Piece of the Last Chapter
(This novella is completely fiction)

It began, the end of this journey, the end of this last piece of this chapter with a jet ride and a prayer for those lost during the middle passage. The jet was headed for an island. Maybe Jamaica or Antigua. Maybe the Caymans or Bermuda.

I was to be a passenger on that jet but I was bumped. That can happen when you are flying standby, however, there was something strange about this jet and the people on it. There might have also been something strange about the jet itself.

Although I was not allowed to board this jet, I observed the people entering the jet. Most of the passengers were white males although their wives accompanied some of these men. Very few had their children. One factor for sure, that was wide spread was the feeling that they were from old money, old wealth, power influence and prestige. They were headed for the same type of fun in the sun that I was; however, they had their tickets.

One unaccompanied white male arrived late; however, he snarled at the ticket agent who spoke politely to several of us with standby tickets. He said "I have a regular ticket and I know you will not allow these standby ticket holders to board before me will you?" The ticket agent quickly gave him a boarding pass.

The boarding process began. I watched the passenger's board the jet wondering if I could be a fly on that jet, what would I see and hear. This jet was headed for Bermuda but would pass over the Caribbean Sea.

Once on board the jet in my disguise, I visited the passengers one by one and noticed that there were some common themes that tied their conversations together. One conversation centered on how these two contractors had used this African-American (Afroan) contractor to obtain a government contract. And once they received the government contract, they plotted against the African-American contractor and dropped him.

Another couple talked about how much they hated affirmative action because the result was that African-Americans was actively competing with whites for jobs whites would receive automatically before. Still yet another conversation centered on how most whites feel that in America, no one owes African-Americans reparations for the millions and billions of dollars of slave labor extracted from the millions of slaves taken from Africa and sold to whites in North, Central and South America. Old money came from slavery.

All of this sick conversation was becoming a bit too much for me when drama began to unfold.

The pilot had strayed too close to an air corridor that led to the Bermuda.

Suddenly African ancestral spirits dressed in African gowns entered the aircraft as dust particles. I could not believe my eyes.

As soon as the particles formed a body, out came these brothers. They walked around the jet however the whites could not see them. Finally, after 10 of these ancestor spirit brothers arrived, they walked forward to the cockpit. Five of these brothers entered the cockpit and identified themselves to the pilots as Malcolm, Denmark Vessy, Emit, Nat Turner and Maceo, a brother who had led a huge slave revolt in Cuba.

These brothers touched the pilot, co-pilot navigator and engineer on their shoulders. As this was done the flight crew passed out and brothers took over the cockpit while the other five walked about the cabin touching the other passengers and in no time, the crew and passengers had passed out.

The brothers in the cockpit took over the guiding of the aircraft as planned right over the Bermuda Triangle. The aircraft under the command of the brothers began a special decent toward a pattern that lead to the edge of an opening. The co-ordinates were unique and had to be followed to the letter.

The craft entered a fold in the earth, which was surrounded by the Atlantic Ocean, Caribbean Sea and a special unknown body of water.

Finally, the jet landed on a huge underwater underground land and taxied to a stop. This place was called African Ancestor spirit World.

The Ancestral soldiers removed the passengers from the plane and put them in old rusty shackles, the types that were used on African slaves all over the Americas.

This land beneath the sea, I had heard about while in Africa, was beautiful. There were great pyramids along wide clean tree lined boulevards and streets. Great monuments were all over the place that bestowed glory to God and to all of the people of the World. Many of these monuments celebrated the heroism of African freedom fighters that were killed trying to free slaves. Slavery in the Americas, the biggest human rights violation even visited upon human kind was totally discredited by huge posters and billboards.

The spirits moved by foot or flight and changed their form when entering their pyramid style homes and buildings. Any time they wanted to, they could project or take on African human forms.

The passengers and the jet were assumed to be missing by the land based air traffic controllers, as search and rescue units or radar did not pick up the jet. It was assumed that craft went down in an unknown destination.

The passengers were brought to the Great Hall of African Ancestral Spirits in chains and shackles. The passengers were making ugly and racist remarks but found resistance useless in this African-Ancestral Spirit Land.

The land took on the form of a large island surrounded by the sea; however, the sea could not enter the land. This was a land of vast wealth, with cars, trucks, buses and bicycles all over the place. Although it was an African ancestral homeland blessed by God, other people were well represented. This was a land of peace, a good example for America to emulate with fairness and justice in place of greed, racism and racist oppression. There was a water front street that made a complete 8-mile circle around parts of this land.

The passengers were brought to the Great Central Hall in a building that could only be described as the greatest pyramid ever built.

The spirit soldiers transported the passengers so as not to cause them pain. The passengers were lined up in a great row of chairs that faced the Ancestral Spirits Council seats located on a great podium above the crew and passenger chairs.

The Spirit Council asked the crew and passengers to select 3 representatives to speak for them in this great ekpe or judgement.

The crew had an easy job. They picked the pilot, co-pilot and engineer. The passengers had a more difficult job and requested the removal of the shackles as well as more time. The African Ancestral Spirit Council after some deliberation decides that the shackles had been left on African slaves for 400 years in North, South, Central America and the Caribbean and these would not be removed; however, more time was granted.

Meanwhile the U.S. Army, Air Force, Navy and Marines mounted joint search and rescue operations. The CIA was also brought into the effort with no success. The jet was reported lost at sea.

Three representatives were chosen by the passengers to represent them before the African Ancestral Spirits Council. The council was finally called into session by the left on African slaves for 400 years in North, South, Central America and the Caribbean and these would not be removed; however, more time was granted.

Meanwhile the U.S. Army, Airforce, Navy and Marines mounted joint search and rescue operations. The CIA was also brought into the effort with no success. The jet was reported lost at sea. Three representatives were chosen by the passengers to represent them before the African Ancestral Spirits Council. The council was finally called into session by the eleven leading spirits, Somora (Africa), Marcus Garvey (at large), David Sibeiko and Steve Biko from South Africa, Nat Turner, (slaves) Malcolm African -American, Kwame Nkrumah from Ghana, Maceo from Cuba, Brother Lumpkin and a nameless unknown slave from Brazil, Toussiant from Haiti and Patrice Lamumba of the Congo.

Each of them spoke pointing an accusing hand at a racist white America, about the racism of slavery during reconstruction and up to today's racism which continues to be as destructive if not as brutal.

The passengers and crew representatives appealed to have the chains removed one by one. Malcolm responded from the Council. Who will remove the shackles of white racism from my brothers and sisters in America? The Caribbean, Central and South America?

The crew and passengers representatives responded one by one. We do not represent our government or the governments of any of these other countries who are accused of white racism or of mistreatment representatives turned their head down saying not me.

Samora asked who will pay reparations to Africa for the pillage and plundering of colonialism? Again no answer came from the representatives that could be creditable. Next, the Brazilian unknown slave spoke up and said who will pay reparations to Brazilian and other Africans who were enslaved in South America? Again no credible answer came from the representatives.

Toussiant of Haiti spoke up next saying what about the rape and plunder of my country and the brothers and sisters in the Caribbean. Who will pay reparations for the suffering of my people? The French? The British? Again no reply came from the representatives

Finally, Patrice Lumumba spoke up for East and Central Africa including the Congo with a brief but specific question preceded by a powerful statement. He said I was brutally killed by forces of the old and new colonialism. The West and African puppets joined together with the UN and IMF (international Monetary Fund) mob to torture and kill me. Why should we not do the same to you?

There was a big commotion among the passengers. There was a big discussion among the crew and passenger representatives and how to answer that question. Before an answer could be given, Steven B. and David Sabeiko rose up and backed up what Lamumba said, saying we were also victims of the oppressive forces and our people were slaughtered. Our country suffered some of the worst oppression since none of you think you should take any responsibility for what you have done why should you now be spared?

Brother Samora then rose up and said you Know that I am fed up because western forces shot down my jet and plundered my people a second time 500 years after the original colonial disaster. I wonder if you should be spared?

Brother Lumpkin raised up and said I was killed by two San Francisco policeman while I was trying to give myself up however I was only one of thousands of African-American victims of police/ prison guard brutality and murder of Blacks by whites. I say you owe reparations or at least a serious effort to make it happen.

The representatives of the passengers and crew were ready to respond. The pilot said, well I must admit that that my people have done a lot of evil deeds to African People all over the world. However I know our race will never atone for these great crimes and the other whites will make the passengers and crew regret attempting to promote reparations. And besides, even though the crew and passengers have personally benefited from these atrocities, we will bear no responsibilities and feel we should be allowed to continue our journey.

The Navy, Air Force Coast Guard, National Security Administration, CIA and other American Forces continued to search for the lost 747 full of old money elites. Despite those efforts the jet was not seen on radar, satellite or other tracking apparatus.

Suddenly A prominent African spirit rose up Brother M, and addressed the African Spirit Council. He spoke in slow but measured tones saying that not until 80 to 90 % of white America was ready to apologize to all Africans the way Bill Clinton apologized to America about his affair with Monica Lewinsky would the time be right for a real discussion about the reparations owed to Africans is America(African-Americans) and Africans throughout the world.

Martin began to speak again saying yes white America owes a tremendous amount of responsibility however this council has given the passengers and crew a choice and they have refused to accept responsibility.

Martin then urged the council to retire to its chambers for further discussions while the African guard held those on trial. The deliberations were sharp and detailed however after 5 days in spirit time the council decided to allow the jet to return to American air space unharmed with this story firmly embedded in the minds of the passengers and crew. The point had been made.

The lost jet suddenly appeared on the radar screen of the air traffic controllers. The ignorance of the KKK and their supporters had been exposed. The GREAT REPARATIONS DEBATE had been started. The connection between Africa and African-Americans remained strong. A spirit member called for an 8th and 9 th Pan African Congress in a peaceful and democratic Nigeria to discuss reparations for all Africans through out the world in 2002.

Updater of Journey to the Motherland 01 16 2017

Well I have finally relocated the original file of this book so I could add this update.

My Trip to London, England July10, to July12, 2015 Published 12 29 2016 Please visit my new Web Site: www.lovingblackwomen.com/home/

Written by Larry Ukali Johnson-Redd

Well I enjoyed a few days in London on an all expense paid trip as a result of my 4 years teaching experience I had in Nigeria from Nov 1977 until August 1981. While in Nigeria, I only taught at one school namely Eghosa Grammar School located along what was then called New Lagos Road in Benin City, Nigeria. The school was named Eghosa Grammar School and was funded by the government while I was there. Thank you for flying me to London and I say that to all my former students from Eghosa Grammar School. But I also extend that thank you to all students I have taught in America as well.

Since I left Nigeria in sort of a hurry and school was out of session, I really did not have a time to say good bye to my students at Eghosa the only high school I taught at while I lived in Nigeria. My students remembered me and after holding their 3rd convention with the U.S. and Brittan, a decision was made to invite me to London, England July 10th to July 12th, 2015. I will always be grateful to Africa, Nigeria and the Nigerian students I taught in Nigeria.

A few students of mine have contacted me by email over the years like Hilton Idahosa who I saw in London and Femi Aluya who contacted me by email and facebook. The few that reached me all remembered I did not say good bye to them. The ex-student I remember receiving e-mail from and saw at the convention was Hilton Idahosa.

One first of my old Eghosa students was Attorney Henry Omoregie who still lives and works in Benin City. However I also ran into the students who got us checked into our rooms.

The first night at about 6 PM on Friday we all met up in the hospitality room that was as big as 2 big rooms. There was a big feast on adjoining tables of Nigerian food. Since my late wife used to cook for me I had not seen such a big variety of my favorite Nigerian food. There was Egusi full of green veggies as well as Soup and Eba, Abono(drip) Soup, Fried Plain tine, Rice and chicken stew, there were what Nigerians called local beans in a big pot. There was another pan full of Moi Moi which is steam cooked patties of black eyed peas, like a bean cake with chicken, beef and at times boiled eggs inside. There were platters of chicken and beef. When I arrived at the hotel my older brother Darnell and I had a British –boring food lunch. However at the hospitality room I was in heaven on earth with all of my favorite Nigerian foods in a great feast. After two plates, I was full and the rest of the night I met and spoke with my grown ex students who were some 5 to 12 years younger than me. You see I was 25 years old when I arrived in Nigeria.

I have had other students send me e-mails over the years. And many said they discovered me on Face book. I taught government from the heart with many references to Nigeria, Africa, USA, as well as the history of harsh mistreatment of African-Americans and of the Africans in the Caribbean, Central as well as South America. To some of my students I was the first African American man they met. But not all of my students:\because I met another brother from California who was 6 feet 9 inches" while resident in Benin City, Nigeria; when I lived there. This other brother was a national basketball coach. That Charles brother introduced me to Lee Evans, who was a national track coach in Nigeria working mainly in Lagos but a frequent visitor to Benin City. Yea, I mean the track Olympian who protested in the Mexico City Olympics in 1968.

Many of those students told me in London, they remembered my passion i.e., the nationwide oppression and discrimination against my people in the west including America. However many also decided to travel to Britain, the rest of Europe and the East Coast of America to study and even live oversees or study to make it better. One of my ex students Douglas lives in Sacramento, California. Let us be reminded, I taught in Nigeria some 35-38 years ago. How my students remembered me is like magic from that that long ago. I love and respect all of my students from (now named) Eghosa Anglican Boys High School however all of those conventioneers from or associated with Eghosa wrapped me up with great memories, strong respect and African brotherly love.

There were many hugs, handshakes and pictures taken in London including 5 video clips taken by my senior brother and best photographer, I know Darnell Redd who accompanied me on my trip to London. There were a lot of my book (paperbacks) Journey to the Motherland, from San Francisco to Benin City that were sold, donated and autographed while the convention provided a basis for re-opening the Amazon Kindle e-book by the same name adding details of this London trip to the story as an update. The update to Journey to the Motherland will be put together in the next 30 days (Unpacking has taken nearly 2 years.) I taught government in Eghosa School in Benin City in 1977 to 1981. This convention was superbly organized. And I felt truly honored.

Now in 2015 my Nigerian students have remembered me from 37 to 38 years ago. They have given me an expenses paid trip to their 40th annual convention and showered me with love and respect. I will like to thank all of my ex-students and Eghosa Anglican Boys High School itself where I taught.

Here are some of my homies and my older brother, Darnell's homies from Lakeview-San Francisco, CA in 2013.

Larry with the First Tuesday Spoken Word Series Sisters on 3rd Street in San Freancisco

Also I urge the supporters of the current Eghosa-High School and their many supporters in their struggle with the Edo State Government/ Governor to give back the half of the campus that was waterlogged while I taught there. Rumor has it the Governor/ his supporters want to keep this valuable piece of land and share the land into plots to be shared among them rather than give that disputed land back to the school the land was taken from.

My name is Larry Ukali Johnson-Redd. I have written 6 books so far Journey to the Motherland, From San Francisco to Benin City. This book is a paperback you can write me at ljredd52@aol.com.

All 6 of my book, are available as e-books at the Amazon.com/ kindle Web Site. I will expand Journey to the Motherland Journey to the Motherland from San Francisco to Benin City to include a full report on my trip to London including text, video and photos. I will also open an independent Web Site soon. Now is the time to buy Journey to the Motherland as an e- book so when you complete the read of this book, the addition of details from my London Trip will automatically appear in the e-book version. The cost of Journey to the Motherland, from San Francisco to Benin City at Amazon.com/kindle is $2.99. My e-books can download to any country on Earth to your cell, computer or other media in 60 seconds.

Two "Journey to the Motherland, from San Francisco to Benin City" Reviews

BOOK REVIEW by Veronica Brown Printed in the African Times Newspaper based in Los Angeles, California 03/17/03: Journey To The Motherland, From San Francisco To Benin City—Nigeria, written by Larry Ukali Johnson-Redd

Journey to the Motherland:

From San Francisco to Benin City

Larry Ukali Johnson-Redd

If you are looking for some enlightenment, read this book Journey To The Motherland, From San Francisco To Benin City by Larry Ukali Johnson-Redd. It is a revelation of one man's insight and involvement in the political arena of racism towards Black students in this country especially in the 60's and sadly to say still continues in today's society not only in the South but also in the West. The struggles, hardships they had to endure in order to obtain a decent education to better their lives in comparison to their white counterparts.

The first chapter opens with him and his wife returning from the motherland and in one solitude moment on the plane his thoughts flashes back to his youth in the city of San Francisco where he was born.

(This is Chris Okuonghae and I below during a break in the convention in London. Imagine that I taught Chris high school government in Benin City's Eghosa Grammar School in Nigeria between 1977 and 1981. And here we are again is 2014. WOW!!!!!!!)

The next three or four chapters tell you of his days in junior and senior high school. His problems at securing a job was not with (out) its complications, event though his credentials were impressive and impressive they were however he persevered and conquered.

When both he and his wife accepted new posts in Africa, he as a teacher and she to work for the government, it was the most important decision any two people in love with each other could have made. For his wife, it was the best thing that could have happened because she was returning to her country of her birth and he was going there for the first time to his <u>Homeland.</u> The description of places and the cities he visited and most of all the people of Africa were awe-inspiring one only had to close their eyes and you can feel, hear and smell all the *beauty and the sufferings that made Africa the great Continent she is and then you are suddenly transported there.*

(This is Alex Osunde whom I met in London but who graduated before I arrived in Nigeria.)

His description of family greetings, the meeting of old friends and the making of new friends and the making of new ones was something to treasure for a lifetime. While living in Africa he gives one the feeling that you never want leave once you get there, it was like coming home to heaven on earth, His time spent there was the most remarkable of his life with his wife along his side could not have completed a better picture. Much as he loved Africa, he still longed to be back home in America where his family still lived. He returned only to lose his wife and settled back to life in America.

* African American author and activist, LARRY UKALI JOHNSON–REDD

The Writer-Activist

Thoughts of Larry Ukali

Larry Ukali Johnson-Redd is simply a bagful. His name is afrocentric in Look. While his progenitors may have been slave to a Mr. Redd some 400 years ago, Larry finds comfort in his traditional African middle name-Ukali.

The God of mercy has equally been kind to this African American. His looks. Nothing about his looks suggests he is American. His oblong face, his cross-breed nose and those thin and silky hairs on Larry's head all combine to give him away as a Nigerian of the Fulani stock. This resemblance is complete when he tries to smile, and he does smile always. Those slim-chiseled set of teeth, they are unmistakingly Hausa-Fulani.

At first contact, Larry Ukali makes an impression on you. He is full of life, always himself, he has honed his American accent so well it has obliterated the derogatory Black American slang that is ever seeking for shortened version of every word. In the course of the interview which followed our initial meeting at the office of the Editor-in-Chief of this newspaper, Mr. Johnson-Redd uttered the word 'gonna' just once. Amazing!

Another surprise is that Larry pronounces traditional Nigerian names and places with a finesse that will leave many indigenes hiding their faces in shame. From Zaria, Benin, Nkwerre and 'Kedu' the Ibo word for 'How, And the sweetest Ibo words in the mouth of Larry are Chinwe and Uzoma. Names of the author's late wife.

These skills were not acquired in the backyard of San Francisco, Larry's home in America. They were learnt on the streets of Bening City where the activist lived for fours years from 1977 when he first came to Nigeria.

A glorious 24 years has passed since Ukali left Nigeria. But, he is back again. This time, he is not gropping in the dark about where he should go or not. Even without the company of a wife, Larry can find his way about town. And he says this is a greater Nigeria that he has returned to. Larry spoke with DENNIS ONWUEGBU in his Hotel room in Lagos. Excerpts:

Welcome back home, Larry. What brought you this time? I came back for a couple of reasons. One I haven't been to Nigeria for 24 years, I have a vacation, and there is one young lady I want to have further discussion with. These three reasons are uppermost in my mind. Moreto, this is an opportunity for me to write journey two. A sequel to my first book, Journey to the Motherland: From San Francisco to Benin City.

Compared with the first time you came to Nigeria, what difference is there now?

The biggest difference I've seen so far is how I entered the country. It was

Pg. 38

> **❝**
> *At first contact, Larry Ukali makes an impression on you. He is full of life, always himself, he has honed his American accent so well it has obliterated the derogatory Black American slang that is ever seeking for shortened version of every word. In the course of the interview which followed our initial meeting at the office of the Editor-in-Chief of this newspaper, Mr. Johnson-Redd uttered the word 'gonna' just once. Amazing!*
> **❞**

"Journey To The Motherland–
From San Francisco to Benin City"
Novel by Larry Ukali Johnson-Redd
Review By Kola Thomas

San Francisco, CA
This autobiographical "Journey To The Motherland" is a 160- page novel, but I read it in less than two days. Reading this book was an invocation of the nostalgia to be "at home right now." This book is written in a style that helps the reader to be transported to Africa and be actively engaged in the dynamic and evolving events of the moment as they unfold. One could not help but follow the "Journey..." and soak in the moments. Perhaps being a Yoruba (born in Nigeria), familiar with the local terrain and socio-cultural manifestations and political landscape of Nigeria; and living in the Bay Area for over twenty-five years — well I travel home periodically - I am able to understand the book better. However, this is a book about a wonderful experience in Africa.

One thing that is clear throughout the book is a commitment by the author Ukali Johnson-Redd, to increasing empowerment for African people all over the world.

It behooves any one contemplating a visit to any part of Africa; to read "Journey..." A great many brothers and sisters go to Africa, without preparation or some form of orientation. They then experience cultural shock on arrival - shock at the mass of black people taking care of business; shock at the unparalleled and unqualified show of hospitality displayed by the hosts; shock at the high level of intellectual capacity and scholarship; shock at the fact that people are unfazed at whether or not utilities work; and shock at the fact that the urban and rural areas are just as any you will find in the so-called civilized western cities.

I could not help but be thankfully amazed at how Brother Ukali has assimilated the local lingo and nuances to a "T." Talk about "invigilation..." for proctoring a student test - page 124; and dispensing "dongoyaro" – a traditional herbal extract - as the preferred medication for malaria - page 144 - that follows age- long African understanding of traditional therapy – and which Western medicine refuses to celebrate. Perhaps Ukali needs to consider sharing his experience at medical colleges here in the United States.

"Journey to Motherland..." is recommended and a definite must read by every one who wishes to get a better understanding of Africa and African ways, its indubitable and welcoming hospitality, and its great culture, educational environment. Kola Akintola-Thomas is CEO of African Global Institute-USA based in San Francisco, California. He can be reached at africanglobal@yahoo.com

From: ljredd52 <ljredd52@aol.com>
To: ibosa <ibosa@aol.com>
Sent: Tue, Jul 14, 2015 11:18 am
Subject: Re: Hello Ibosa my brother

Hello Ibosa,

This will be a short note of thanks and gratitude to you and the Eghosa Global Alumni Association. Thank you for everything. Guess what? We are now joined at the hip!!!!!! We are together. Your convention took place in an open and democratic fashion. I thought I was in one of my Government classes at Eghosa Grammar School. And this ever so polite convention confirmed a constitution despite many views being expressed initially and throughout the sessions. I also appreciate the love and genuine respect accorded to my senior brother and I. I loved seeing every one and how well you all turned out.

These are immediate thoughts I have while I am unpacking this trip to London. I look forward to communicating with everyone I met or met again at this special 4th Convention. You have my permission to forward this email to all attendees at the convention so they may know how grateful I am for the invitation and their donations. I will eventually correspond with everyone I have a card from however; I would like to be in touch with the entire Eghosa family.

Sincerely,

Larry Ukali Johnson-Redd
925 529 7660

This is Ibosa and I in the convention

Dr Odenefe John Islwea, a well qualified London medical doctor, and chair of Eghoba Global's, the Eghosa Grammar School alumnae-London Chapter leader in 2014

Larry Ukali Johnson-redd
I completed writing the first draft of part 2 of my Obama book

Mobile Uploads · Sep 13 ·
Tag Photo · View Full Size · Make Profile Picture · Edit Photo · Send as Message

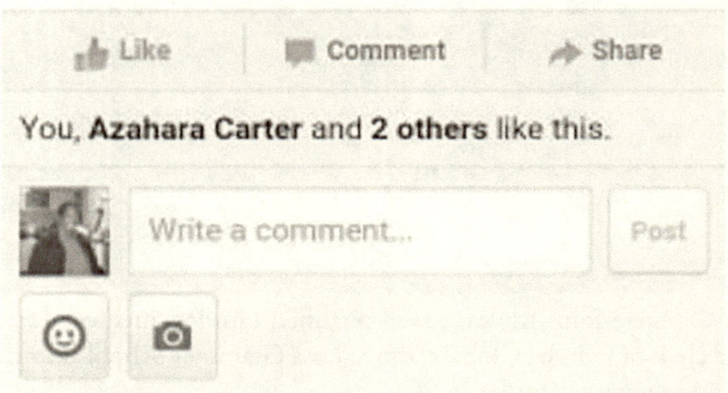

Alex Osunde's review of Journey to the Motherland, From San Francisco to Benin City By Larry Ukali Johnson-Redd
The E-book version is available at Amazon.com/kindle

It was a pleasure meeting you at the Eghoba Convention in London. Thanks for signing my copy of your book. I have since read it over and over.

Yours is an excellent story on what isn't right about the relationship between Africans in the diaspora and those in the motherland. This has created a lot of mutual suspicion and an identity crisis leading to unattainable potential for the race. Your intervention is a timely addition to the literature on the subject. We appreciate your personal sacrifice restoring the dignity of the African over the years. Our condolences on the loss of your soul mate, Chinwe.

Best regards.
Alex Osunde

Special Note:
I graduated in June 1974 from Eghosa Anglican Grammar School, Benin-City. I had left school before you came to teach in Eghosa.

Reviews of History To Destiny Through Afrocentry Poetry

The words in this book made my heart sing. This is because this book gives much needed <u>information</u> on the African experience and what we have lost over the years. Ukali's respect for the Black woman of African descent pays homage to those who have endured so very much. It is apparent that this man was raised by a loving set of parents. I feel that History to Destiny through Afrocentric Poetry should be in every classroom, not only for <u>children</u> of the Diaspora but for others as well. The d-boys standing on the corners of the Black communities would benefit greatly from the words that this brother has penned in such an eloquent fashion. I recommend this book to all who read and to be read to all those who cannot.--Cati A. Hawkins-Okorie, Social Activist

In my reading of History to Destiny Through Afrocentric Poetry I found these poems that radiated with the spirit, and echo the voice and cry of our elders and ancestors, expressed as a conscious priority for Africans in America to unite with Africans in the Diaspora.-- Nashid Ahmad, Grassroots Activist and Spiritual Metaphysics Sun Rise December 1939 Sunset June 26,2011 Rest in Peace!

The three decade-plus of poetry presented in this book by brother Larry Ukali Johnson-Redd speaks to the African mind, and challenges readers to consider a protracted dedication to love and human development.--Itibari M. Zulu, Th.D., President, African American Library and Information <u>Science</u> Association

Over the years I have known Ukali, he has been a consistent advocate for justice and equality for African people everywhere. In this book, History to Destiny Through Afrocentric Poetry, Ukali chronicles his lifetime experiences in America and Africa, and pays homage to our ancestors Langston Hughes, Marcus Garvey, Bob Marley, Marvin Gaye, and many others.

Ukali speaks of solidarity with African people throughout the Diaspora from Lagos to Granada and all points in between. He reflects on our lives, loves, and struggles against racism, oppression and brutality. But most importantly, he has eloquently captured in these pages the righteousness and victory of our struggle as an oppressed people in this the fifth century since enslavement.

In the tradition of a true Griot, Ukali passes on the ancient practice of putting us in touch with these other, our roots, our blackness, and our birthright so we can renew our commitment to ourselves, and our people. . . . I am sure after reading this book you will discover a man whose love of our people will undoubtedly serve to awaken the sleeping giant in us all.--Donald Lacy, Love Life, Don't Take Life -Kpoo.com and KPOOFM San Francisco Wake Up Saturday Morning Radio Show.

I have 6 e-books on sale at Amazon.com namely, Journey to the Motherland, a paperback (COSTS $2.99) 170 pages- History to Destiny Through Afrocentric Poetry released in a limited edition massive paperback of spoken word recently released as an expanded and updated e-book ONLY $2.99 CENTS. Loving Black Women a 130 paged paperback that sold out has also been expanded with several more Black Romance and Love Poems- AN E-BOOK COSTING ONLY $2.99 CENTS. The NEWEST TWO BOOKS are Long Distance Love 220 pages, a memoir about my 4+ year engagement to a Nigerian sister from 2003 to 2008 ($4.49) .American Challenges In The Obama Era Part 1 is my latest book ($2.99).Check out my page at amazon.com/kindle by typing Larry Ukali Johnson-Redd in the Amazon.com/kindle e-book search box. American Challenges in the Obama Era Part 2 is now published and available for purchase during the 2016 time period. Read Part 1 and now Part 2. Thank you if you have read any of my books before or for going to Amazon.com/kindle and reading for the first 10 pages of any of my e-books free.
Check me out on Facebook or Twitter at Ukalitheafricanor or at instagram or linked in.

Here is the link to my newest book at Amazon.com/kindle that costs only $2.99 and views the first 10 pages for free. There is a 2016 Presidential election- guide near the conclusion.
https://www.amazon.com/American-Challenges-Obama-Era-Part-ebook/dp/B01KD6EYAC/ref=sr_1_2?s=fiona-hardware&ie=UTF8&qid=1471199739&sr=8-2&keywords=american+challenges+in+the+Obama+Era

Sincerely,
Larry kali Johnson-Redd
PS Brothers and sisters as well as the New Majority and Progressive readers I ask for your support. Please buy 1 or all of my reasonably priced books.

United States of Africa or Peoples Republic of Africa Read about it in American Challenges in the Obama Era Part 1.

amazon.com/kindle -check it

AMERICAN CHALLENGES in the OBAMA ERA
PART 2
My e-books at amazon.com /kindle
Larry Ukali
Johnson-Redd

www.ingramcontent.com/pod-product-compliance
Lightning Source LLC
Chambersburg PA
CBHW030145010826
48973CB00002B/736